Moral Compass

GOING PLACES

MARINA SKYE

Moral Compass
by Marina Skye

Copyright © 2024 Marina Skye

Mile Marker 1:
Road Trip

Aria raked her long, light brown hair back into a hair tie and huffed a grunt as she tossed her luggage bag into the back of her yellow Mustang GT convertible. It slid sideways against the black leather seat. With country music blaring through the speakers, she let the wind unravel her hair. The horn was honking as she pulled up along the curb in front of Michelle's little town house.

"Yeah, yeah, I'm comin'!" Michelle hollered, dragging her heavy suitcase out of the front door with both hands.

"You bringing a whole log cabin?" Aria shouted.

"Pretty much. You know me," Michelle answered, laughing.

Aria got out of the car and popped open the trunk before helping Michelle put her luggage in.

"Whooo! I'm so excited!" Michelle fixed her curly blonde messy bun and jumped over the car door, sliding into the passenger seat.

"Me too! I *so* need this vacation. Two weeks of traveling, seeing new places, spending time with friends...it's going to be great." Aria pulled the flannel button-up shirt that hung from her waist tighter before getting back into the driver's seat. As they pulled away and drove down the street, Michelle asked, "So work has been that stressful lately, huh? More than usual?"

Aria nodded and answered in a somber tone, "Yeah. When the kids have good days it's so much easier, for me *and* them. There have been too many not so good days lately. We lost two this week; two that I had gotten really close to, and I know I'm not supposed to get too close to the patients but it's hard not to, ya know?"

"Oh, yeah, for sure. You care for them every day. I can imagine how tough it is for you. I'm so sorry." Michelle laid a caring hand on Aria's shoulder.

"Thanks. I decided to take this vacation because I want to enjoy life right now, in the moment, carefree. We only live once and every day I'm reminded how short it can be."

"That's true."

"A couple of years ago, there was this boy, nine or ten years old, who was in remission from leukemia. He had been my favorite patient for well over a year. He told me, 'You have to be happy in whatever you do. Go on adventures once in a while, try new things, get lost in a book or just feel the wind in your hair to feel alive.' I'll never forget him saying that."

"Did that boy's story have a happy ending?"

"It did. He came to the hospital to see me a few months ago and brought me flowers. He was wearing a black Stetson that a friend gifted him for his birthday. The little gentleman said he's a cowboy now and has worn that hat every single day since it was given to him and that he tried something new that made him happy along with recently learning to play guitar. He was making every day feel like an adventure. Then he winked and gave me the biggest hug."

"Aww, that's adorable. What a kid!" Michelle pressed her hand over her heart.

"He is quite a kid. Wise for such a young soul. He's one of those that touches every heart he comes across. Unforgettable. I'm so glad I was lucky enough to have gotten to know him and that he's doing so well. I wish they all had outcomes that were positive. I promised him I'd take time for myself."

"Absolutely. I wish life was fair. Well, we're going to take that

2

kid's advice on this trip. We're going to experience it all. Until you drop us off at Shellee's." Michelle laughed.

"Heart-racing adventures!" Aria laughed at herself. "Who am I kidding? I'm scared of everything."

"We'll still have fun. Whooo!" Michelle flung her arms in the air, Aria following suit, feeling the wind's resistance against their skin and their hair blowing around in the wind.

The girls pulled into Jade's driveway as Jade and LeShea came running out, duffle bags in-hand like they were robbing a bank, and tossed them into the back seat before leaping in.

"Let's hit the road, bitches!" Jade shouted as loudly as her soft-spoken voice could.

"Drive it like ya stole it!" LeShea gave the side of the car a double tap and tossed her head back laughing, making the girls cackle as those wide tires squealed out, heading west for several miles before stopping for gas.

"Any idea where we're exploring first?" Jade asked, getting out of the car as Aria popped the gas cap off.

"No idea. Thought we were winging it?" LeShea shrugged as Aria hit the unleaded button and started pumping gas while Michelle stepped out of the car and slipped her shoes on.

"Snack or drink preferences?" Jade asked.

"Nah, y'all go on in, I'll be right behind ya."

"Suit yourself." LeShea adjusted the bottom of her t-shirt as she and Jade walked into the gas station.

"I might as well at least go in to pee." Michelle followed.

As Aria screwed the gas cap back on and opted for no receipt, a white Jeep pulled in and up to the next pump. She heard a dog bark from the Jeep as she was entering the store.

The girls had their arms full of snacks and Jade was slurping a slushie when Aria walked in. Aria quickly grabbed a couple of drinks and snacks and headed to the counter behind the girls. They headed back out to the car together, passing a man along the way. The girls were talking as they dug drinks from the bag, distracting Aria before she turned to check him out, unable to see his face as he walked in the opposite direction. That five-liter motor revved up and the girls drove off, the image of that guy's nice ass still in Aria's head.

"Once we hit I-40, we can hit some popular Route 66 spots," Aria suggested.

"I'm looking forward to the food," Michelle blurted, Jade nodding in agreement.

"If you ladies see somewhere you wanna stop, just holler, otherwise I'm going to keep driving till I hit the highway."

"You sure the 'stang is reliable enough for this road trip? She's not very new." Jade seemed worried.

"Hey, now. Are you kidding? The '94 is the best body style in my opinion and the last year of the true five-liter. I had her tuned up and got her an annual checkup. She's ready to rev these RPMs on a wide-open road, running free."

"As long as she makes it to Shellee's, that's all that matters," Michelle joked.

"That may be what matters to you girls, but I'll still have a week of traveling after I drop y'all off at her house. I can't believe you two get to stay longer and don't want to finish the loop back with me."

"Hey, plane tickets were cheap and one-way to Oklahoma is going to be long enough to ride in a car," Michelle said.

"Yeah, you're crazy if you think we're just driving for two weeks straight," LeShea agreed.

"Making stops along the way though." Aria shrugged.

"Still. I'd rather spend an extra day at Shellee's and then fly back," Michelle said.

"You gonna be okay on your own though?" Jade asked.

"Me? Pfft. Hello, have you met me?"

"Yeah, that's what we're sayin'." Jade laughed.

"Seriously, I'll be just fine."

"Now I kinda feel bad." LeShea pouted playfully.

"Well, don't, really. This will be good for me. I could use some time alone honestly."

"You're just trying to make us feel better." Michelle rubbed Aria's shoulder.

"Nah. I knew you two had flights booked ahead of time and I still chose to take the full two week vacation. A week just isn't long enough."

"I admire that deep adventurous soul of yours but mine isn't quite as deep." Jade laughed.

"It's something you should do for yourself, for sure. We just want you to stay safe." Michelle tilted her head in concern.

"I will. I'm always alert and aware of my surroundings. Just me, music, fresh air, and the open road for sight-seeing; it'll be great."

"Well, we'll make this week together a memorable one." LeShea's wide smile was a mischievous one.

"Damn right we will. I need this time to find a new direction for myself."

"What do you mean?"

"I've always been on the straight and narrow. Life has been clean-cut. Every day is practically the same. I need to experience unplanned spontaneity. I need to relax and enjoy myself, do random stuff that I've never done. I just wanna let loose but stick to my morals too, ya know?"

"I get it. You deserve it too. You work too much and what you do for work is emotionally draining." Michelle applied lipstick using the visor mirror.

"I just need to go somewhere, anywhere, any place other than work or home. I have a spontaneous urge to go someplace new, out of my comfort zone. Looking forward to trying new foods even."

"You girls getting hungry?" Jade asked, always up for a food run.

"Yep!" Michelle wasn't one to turn down food.

"Fast food? Or we wanna stretch our legs?" Aria asked, looking at a road sign.

"Grease in a go-sack is fine with me if it'll get us to the adventure faster," LeShea said.

"Food stops can be an adventure too." Jade smiled.

"True. Let's hit some famous places when we hit Route 66," Michelle suggested.

"Wish we were going through New Orleans. I could go for some Cajun food." LeShea was a musician groupie, often following her favorite artists, so she knew her way around that city.

"Ooh, and some beignets too!" Michelle clapped her hands in excitement.

"That does sound good. Let's do it. We're taking I-10 over to 20, then we'll go up 55 and hit 40." Aria gave in easily.

"Sweet! I mean, we're going through Mobile now anyway, it's really not much farther." Jade quickly adjusted their route on her phone.

Mile Marker 2: Cajun Food & Onward... or Not

While passing through New Orleans, the girls ate a Cajun meal on Bourbon Street and grabbed a side of powdered sugar beignets and ate them on the steps facing Jackson Square, watching people and horse-drawn carriages before taking a stroll down by the river to watch boats float by. Then onward they traveled, northbound through Jackson, Mississippi to Memphis, Tennessee, where they danced in the streets to musicians performing on sidewalks before retreating to a tranquil treehouse resort in the mountains. White lights were strung along the wooden sidewalks. The atmosphere was perfect for relaxing and it was the best night sleep Aria had gotten in a long time. They did, however, get woken up by birds chirping happily early the next morning, so their day began earlier than expected. On their way through Arkansas, they drove through the Ozark St. Francis National Forest that runs along the Arkansas River. They hiked to take scenic photos from cliffs overlooking the green hills and valleys, stopping at rushing waterfalls along the way, watching fishermen through the pines and oaks as they took in the fresh air. On a whim, they hiked a two-hour trail excursion over rocky bluffs and across mountain streams. The terrain was a bit rough for Mustang tires, so they took it slow heading out to the interstate, but about ten miles later on I-40, the car felt as though it was vibrating.

"You feel that?" Michelle asked from the passenger seat.

"I feel it," Jade confirmed.

Aria turned down the music they had been singing along to just in time for a loud pop sound. She handled the car well and pulled over to the shoulder of the road as black rubber pieces trailed behind them.

"Well shit!" Aria slammed her fist on the steering wheel, frustrated.

"You have a spare?" LeShea asked, getting out of the car.

"Yeah, but only one so I hope only this one tire was damaged. Dammit, I just bought these tires too." Aria got out and kicked the blown tire. She popped the trunk and lifted the false bottom before taking the tire out. She looked for the jack while LeShea held the floor of the trunk up for her.

"I don't see one. I thought I had everything I needed. How is it not in here?" Aria set the spare full-sized tire at her feet and leaned it against the car as she kept digging in the trunk. "My tool kit is gone too. Shit!"

"Well prepared, huh?" Jade giggled, tongue in cheek.

Aria let out a sigh. "I remember taking it out in my driveway and setting it to the side to rearrange for more luggage room. I guess I forgot to put it back in. Ugh!"

"You have roadside service?" LeShea asked, hands on her hips, as she watched traffic rush by.

"I think so. The number is in the glovebox." She had Michelle hold the tire to keep it from rolling and walked to the passenger side.

"Someone's stopping to help," Jade pointed out, shielding her eyes with her forearm.

Aria was bent over digging through her glovebox when LeShea said, "Hot damn!"

Aria stood and turned, the business card in her hand falling to the ground as she laid eyes on a hella handsome man walking toward them from his white Jeep. Her jaw hung loose as it seemed he was walking in slow motion out of a movie.

"Is he a mirage?" she asked.

"Nope. I see him too," Michelle said, lowering her sunglasses on her nose and watching him above the rims.

Aria felt her heart start to race as he approached. It was the man with the nice ass from the gas station. His dark, curly, chin-length hair and clean trimmed facial scruff gave him a uniquely rugged look. She noticed his perfect complexion and smooth skin. His snug navy t-shirt went nicely with the khaki joggers and white sneakers he wore. He lifted his dark shaded sunglasses onto the bill of his baseball cap as he peeked around at the blown tire.

"You ladies need a hand?"

There was a pause before Aria answered, "Sure, if you don't mind. I have changed a tire before."

"She doesn't have a jack though," Jade said as Aria tugged at the bottom of Jade's shirt to shush her, smiling.

"I can help with that. Give me a second." He walked back to the Jeep, which was only about thirty feet behind the Mustang, his shoulders square with perfect posture.

"What?" Jade whispered, jerking herself away from Aria's grip as Aria kept staring at him, senses heightened.

"So, that's why you have a thing for guys in Jeeps. I think *I* do too now," LeShea joked.

Aria didn't comment but was fighting a smile pretty damn hard. She watched him until he turned back toward them, jack in one hand and tool-kit in the other.

"We appreciate you stopping to help," Aria said as he hiked the thighs of his pants and knelt down by the tire.

"Sure. I figure it's faster than calling for roadside assistance." His brown eyes looked up at Aria, sending a shock wave through her. She realized she must have been staring blatantly at him with her jaw loose as he flashed a perfect white smile before cranking the jack up under the car.

Aria cleared her throat. "It's faster, I'm sure. I'm glad I had a full-size tire for a spare."

"Yeah, those donuts aren't ideal for the interstate for too long."

"And we'll be on it for a long haul," Jade said.

Michelle looked at her, signaling for her to not give details of their travels, but she remained oblivious.

"Yeah? Girls' road trip?" he asked, crouched down.

"Yep."

"Nice. I'm on a road trip myself." He cranked the ratchet in his hand, arm muscles flexing and Aria watching his every move.

"Hitting any particular spots? Or are you on a mission to just one destination?" LeShea inquired, leaning her hip against the car in front of him with her arms crossed. He pulled what was left of the old tire off as he said, "Hitting places actually. I have a route planned out."

"Business or pleasure?" she asked.

He looked up at her and adjusted his baseball cap to keep the sun from his eyes.

"Both, I guess." He put the spare tire on and Aria handed him the lug nuts. Michelle tore apart blades of grass, sitting in the grass with her knees up, elbows on her knees. He cranked the ratchet, tightening each bolt and nut.

"So where are you girls headed next?"

"A little bit of everywhere. On a planned loop ourselves," Aria answered, not giving away their plans to a stranger.

He lowered the jack and pulled it out from under the car then brushed his dirty hands off onto his pants and dusted dirt from his knees.

"Well, I wish you all safe travels."

"Thanks. You too...um." Aria held out a hand to shake his.

"Oh! Tripp. Sorry." He shook her hand with his blackened rubber-stained hand.

"Aria. Thanks again for helping us out."

"No problem."

"What do I owe you?"

"Not a thing."

"Oh, come on. Let me pay you something."

"No, ma'am. I appreciate the offer though."

"You sure?"

"Positive. I'll tell ya what. If we run into each other again, you can buy me a coffee or a drink or something." He grinned, knowing full well he wouldn't let her even if their paths were to cross.

"Deal." She was excited at the thought of running into him again.

He nodded but couldn't help letting his eyes quickly wander her body. A loud bark echoed nearby and Aria looked past Tripp as he turned around to see his dog with its head out the passenger window.

"Time to go. Ladies, enjoy your trip." He picked up the jack and toolbox and headed for his Jeep, the brown boxer panting impatiently.

"Thanks, you too!" Aria shouted, kicking a small chunk of rubber over to the grass from the road before they loaded up.

"Ya know, you should've gotten that guy's number. He wasn't wearing a ring," LeShea said.

"You noticed?" Aria asked, brows wrinkled.

"Of course," LeShea and Michelle both answered, Jade nodding her head.

"I didn't. I was looking at everything else. My God, he's a tall drink. I'm certain he is unmatched by any other man on the planet. That athletic build that's obvious through his clothes, and those joggers...they accentuate his perfect ass."

"We know," Jade said, leading the giggles as their hair flew behind them.

"What are the chances of running into him again?" LeShea wondered out loud.

"Hopefully very high," Aria said, her voice wistful as she daydreamed.

"I'll take that bet," Jade said.

"Mmhmm, me too." Michelle had her bare feet up on the dash, tapping them to the beat of the music playing.

After many miles of driving through flat plains, a gas station and an Airstream diner just off the interstate were a breath of fresh air.

"I'm guessing the folks who work here live off that exit we passed a while back. This is seriously in the middle of nowhere." Michelle looked around at the nothingness surrounding them.

"I'm glad this stop randomly popped up because we're almost on empty." Aria slowed and turned in.

After filling up the tank, Airstream diner food was a must, mutually agreed upon. The girls took a booth by the front window when they entered the chrome diner. Red leather seats creaked as they got comfortable.

"Too bad that guy was traveling and doesn't live here." Jade flipped open a menu.

"Why's that? And his name was Tripp, not 'that guy'." Aria chose what she wanted to order and closed her menu, sliding it to the end of the table.

"Eye candy," LeShea mumbled as a waitress came over, pulling the pen from above her ear and smacking her gum as she held a notepad. The girls gave their drink order and the waitress walked back behind the counter to fetch them.

"Mmhmm," Michelle and Jade agreed, nodding.

"We saw the way he looked at you," Jade told Aria.

"Really? I know I was staring at him but I'd shy away when his eyes caught mine. Think he noticed?"

The girls looked at each other and giggled.

"Really? Crap." Aria hung her head. The waitress brought drinks back to the table, took straws from her apron pocket and flopped them on the table before taking their food order.

"What does it matter anyway? You'll probably never see him again." Jade could be blunt. Michelle, who was facing the door, spit her soda out in a short spray and covered her mouth quickly with a napkin. Jade looked over next to her at Michelle, who was looking straight ahead. Jade saw what had Michelle surprised.

"Holy shit! No way!" She clunked her soda down onto the table, Aria and LeShea both turning in the booth to see Tripp walking in. He made his way to the counter to place an order to go.

"Okay, that's a weird coincidence, am I right? Did he follow us?" Aria asked without taking her eyes off him. "He had left ahead of us though."

"Doesn't mean he didn't pull off somewhere," Jade said.

"Yeah, lying in wait like a serial killer." Michelle wiped her soda spray off the table.

"Oh my God, Michelle." Aria laughed.

"What? I watch a lot of horror movies. Documentaries too. I don't wanna be featured in an episode."

"We know, which makes you paranoid," LeShea retorted, staring at Tripp, who was leaning his palms on the counter.

"More like street smart. Come on, it's weird." Michelle wiped her mouth with a napkin.

He turned to lean his back against the counter and saw the girls pretending not to be staring at him. A sideways grin quickly sprouted on his face and he strolled over to say hello.

"Well, hello again, ladies."

"Hello," all three greeted.

"You're welcome to join us," Aria offered for him to have a seat.

"That's kind of you, but I'm grabbing lunch to go. My dog is waiting in the Jeep. Thought I'd ask how that tire is holding up."

"Everything is great. Thank you again." Aria batted shy eyes.

"My pleasure."

"Where are you headed next? Decide yet?" Aria asked, hands moving off the table so the waitress could set food down.

"Not sure yet. I have a route planned but not the stops. Wherever my heart takes me, I guess, or wherever the wind blows." He shrugged and the other waitress at the counter hollered his name, followed by, "Order up!" The dog barked with his head sticking out of the Jeep window.

"That's my cue to hit the road. Well, you ladies have a safe trip. It was nice to have met you all."

"You as well." Aria smiled.

He nodded and returned to the counter to retrieve his food and pay then headed out the door. The girls watched him leave from their window seat.

"Think we'll ever see him again?" Aria sighed, watching the Jeep roll through a dust cloud.

"You're hoping so," LeShea teased.

Aria couldn't fight a smile as she answered, "Absolutely."

"You should've given him your number," Jade said as she slurped the last few drops of her soda through the straw. Aria wore a bummed look on her face.

"Shit! Why didn't I think of that? I owe him a drink too."

"Because you were too busy drooling over him." LeShea reached across the table and stole a fry from Jade's plate.

"I guess I was. Well, I blew that opportunity."

"Go! Run after him!" Michelle slapped Aria's arm, coaxing her to run out the door, against her better judgment.

"Well, if it was meant to be, you'll see him again." Jade, ever the ray of sunshine, was trying to cheer Aria up.

"Yeah, or if he's a serial killer who's stalking us, you'll see him again," Michelle said around a mouthful.

"Oh my God, will you stop? He is not." Aria laughed.

"You don't know that. The world isn't that small." Michelle waved a hand and added a shoulder shrug.

"I have a good sense of intuition. I bet he's a really good guy. Wish I could find out. Ugh, how could I be so stupid?" Aria was being hard on herself, resting her forehead in her hands as her elbows leaned on the table.

"Let's hurry and finish eating. Maybe we can catch up to him." LeShea shoveled in food.

"How would we do that? We don't even know which direction he went." Jade shrugged.

"We don't have a specific direction in which we need to head so...I don't know, maybe take the path most traveled since it would be better odds." Aria's hope was dwindling.

They finished eating quickly, asking for a to-go box eventually and the check. When it arrived, the check had "paid" written at the top and a phone number written at the bottom. The girls looked at the waitress confused; brows turned in as to why the waitress was handing out her phone number.

"Wait...so—" Aria started but the waitress interrupted.

"That gentleman that y'all were chatting with paid your check. Left a little tip too." She winked before walking away.

"See," Jade said, slapping the table. "It was meant to be!"

"Let's roll!" Aria said excitedly as she waved for the girls to slide from the booth and tossed a twenty on the table before shoving the receipt in the go bag.

"It may not be a small world, but I was so happy to see him again, even so briefly," Aria said, starting up the car.

"And to get his number this time too." Jade looked at the receipt she pulled from the bag.

"What? It was...it was *his* number!" Aria realized, LeShea cracking up in the passenger seat. Aria's eyes were huge as she snatched it from Jade to take a closer look. They all squealed with excitement.

"Wait. How do we know who exactly he left it for?" Aria asked.

"Well, you're the one he winked at...both times!" Michelle rolled her eyes playfully. "You were just in a zone, weren't you? Good grief."

"Or maybe he just wanted to hang out with all of us or left it in case we needed help again." LeShea shrugged.

Both Jade and Michelle shook their heads and said, "Nah."

"You really think? He didn't say anything that would indicate that."

"It was the way you two looked at each other. He didn't need to *say* anything," Jade said.

"He was quite smitten with you, Aria," LeShea agreed.

Aria couldn't hide her excitement, her blushing cheeks and gushing smile showed a happiness the girls hadn't seen in her in quite some time.

Aria gave up on holding on to her sunhat as they began flying down the road. She tossed it down to the floor and let the wind whip her hair. The sun pelted down on their bare shoulders, the heat of the day causing no need for more than a tank top.

"I'd make him wait before calling him." LeShea touched up her lipstick in the passenger mirror.

"How long?"

"Why? Did you plan to call him right away?" LeShea put the lid back on her lipstick.

"I guess not. I should make him wonder, huh? But I don't want him getting too far away, either." Aria sounded desperate.

"It's a girls' trip, so we should have fun together," Michelle reminded them.

"Yeah, let's do that. Let's make our loop over to Shellee's, then when we're at her place, I'll give him a call. Or maybe when I leave there."

"What if it's too late? What if he's long gone by then? You should maybe call now," Jade encouraged.

"Then you'll have to get to know each other through social media or something," Michelle said.

"Yeah. I mean, he's traveling and you're traveling so it might be hard to get to know someone on the road when not actually traveling together," Jade pointed out.

"I'd rather get to know him off-road." Aria gave a quick raise of her brows before giggling.

"Speaking of: how about an excursion?" LeShea suggested.

"Yeah, let's find an adventure!" Michelle agreed, clapping her hands.

"I'll look up places nearby," LeShea said, scrolling on her phone. "Red Rock Canyon Park is an option."

"Where is it?" Aria asked, reading road signs as they flashed by.

"Hinton. Not that far."

"You girls feel like taking another hike?"

"Of course!" Michelle was on board.

"Yep, let's do it," Jade agreed.

Mile Marker 3: Red Rock

The girls hiked through the red clay trails, uphill and through dry foliage, looking up wildflower species while taking scenic photos. Aria re-tied her flannel shirt around her waist and set up her phone with a timer for a group photo.

"Is this our last stop before Shellee's place?" Michelle asked as they turned back down the narrow trail.

"I think so. She doesn't live far. Y'all have fun plans for after I leave?" Aria asked.

"Just horseback riding so far. It's so cool she has horses right there at her ranch," LeShea said.

"Horses are that woman's life. I'm sure she knows some great trails. Great restaurants too."

"I am a bit jealous of all the places you plan to see," Jade said, a pouty look on her face.

"That's our fault," Michelle reminded her with a chuckle.

"I know. I do look forward to pics though. Lots of them, from all of you." Aria pointed to each of them.

"Think Tripp will end up in any of yours?" LeShea teased Aria with an elbow bump.

"I doubt it. What are the chances of running into him a third time? Besides, I have shitty luck."

"Third time might be a charm," Jade said, laughing.

"I'm never that lucky. I can't find a decent guy. They're all morally corrupt."

"You've only looked locally though. You're too good for dating sites," Jade said with a nose wrinkle.

"Well, Tripp was nice enough to stop to help us out and generous enough to pay for our meal. I think that screams good guy."

"He's hot too. Bonus!" LeShea shot a quick raise of her brows. Her boy-crazy side came out often.

They clunked dried clay off their sneakers before getting into the car.

"Maybe y'all could finish this road trip together." Jade wore a smirk.

Aria smiled wide at the thought.

"What a *Tripp* that would be." Aria quoted her pun with her fingers as they merged back onto the interstate.

The girls spent three days riding horses and having fun grown-up sleepovers at Shellee's ranch. They spent that last night at a Route 66 bar, dancing and singing their hearts out. The next morning, they sat on the porch overlooking golden fields, coffee mugs in hand, easing hangovers.

"It's a good thing we called a cab last night. I don't remember the drive home." Shellee wiped her eyes with her fingertips.

"I barely do. Was the cab driver cute? I think I remember him being cute," LeShea asked, her nose wrinkled.

"No!" All the girls shook their heads, laughing, except Shellee, who seriously didn't remember.

"He wouldn't have been as cute as Tripp anyway." Aria smiled and looked up at the sky in a daydream.

"She's got it bad," Michelle bantered out the corner of her mouth.

"So, he's that attractive huh?" Shellee asked, knowing that's all Aria could think about.

"Oh, absolutely! He has a unique rugged look about him

unlike any guy I've ever seen. I should've snuck a pic of him but I didn't even think about it."

"Again, you were too busy drooling over him." Jade laughed.

"Googly eyes," LeShea teased, batting hers for dramatic effect.

"I'm sure I made it obvious too," Aria worried, rolling her eyes.

The girls shook their heads no, slowly and sarcastically. Shellee waving it off like it was no big deal, knowing full well she did without having been there to witness it herself.

"Now you girls have me wondering if I was flirting loudly with my face."

"What does it matter? It's almost a certain thing that you will never see that man again...ever."

"Michelle! Rude!" Jade said with a clenched jaw.

"Yeah, twice was just lucky probably," Shellee agreed. "Unless you just call him, already."

"Wonder if you're on his mind as much as he's on yours," Jade pondered aloud.

"A girl can dream. Even with having dream-killers for best friends," Aria laughed as she looked at the time on her phone and stood. "I'll think about calling him, okay?"

"Look. If you do happen to run into him again or plan to meet up," Jade began, pointing a finger at Aria. "Don't let the right one pass you by as you watch someone else snag him up. You'll come across one—hopefully Tripp—that you'll want to get to know more and you'd better make a move. Otherwise, you'll always wonder what might have been. Don't do that to yourself. That would be heartbreaking."

"Thanks for the lecture." Aria rolled her eyes, arms crossed playfully, adding a smile.

"It's advice. We don't want to see you become an old cat lady, alone," Michelle added.

"You know me better than that. I'm more of a dog person." Aria laughed. "Well, girls, I should probably get goin'."

"You sure you don't want to stay longer? I've really enjoyed you being here."

"Well, of course I want to, but with all the stops I plan to make, I'll have to stick to the plan if I want to make it back to work on time at the end of my vacation. Next time, you come stay with us. We'll show ya around."

"Yes! I need to come visit. We understand. We're gonna miss you though." Shellee hopped down from the railing on which she was perched to head back inside.

"Aww, I'll miss you girls too. This has been so much fun. I hadn't been horseback riding in forever. We need to find a place back home to do that."

"I hear great things about Brandton Ranch. We'll have to check it out," LeShea said.

Aria headed inside behind Shellee for her luggage bag, the other girls following. She set her mug in the kitchen sink and rolled her luggage bag to the door.

"Y'all have plans for tonight already?" Aria asked.

"Oh, I don't know. Maybe we'll go to a drive-in movie and let a twister come tearing through."

"Haha, not funny."

"Pffft, you don't know what a good time is then. It doesn't just happen in the movies." Shellee laughed.

"Please be safe and keep us updated." Michelle scowled at Shellee as she helped hold the door open for Aria.

"Yes! Send us pics!" The envy in Jade's voice was barely contained.

"Oh, you can count on that. I have my phone location on too, just in case. I appreciate you girls caring about my safety. I love ya for it." She made her rounds with hugs then the girls followed to the porch.

"We love you, boo! Stay safe and have a blast." Michelle gave Aria the biggest hug then hollered, "Go get that man!" as Aria loaded her bag into the back seat.

"I'll try!" Aria laughed at Michelle's rough, playful tone. "You girls have fun and have a safe flight home. Miss ya already!" She blew them a kiss as she got into the car and revved the engine, giving the princess parade float wave through the cloud of dust kicking up behind the tires as she headed out of the driveway.

Mile Marker 4:
Twisted Fates

Aria was enjoying the drive; top down, wind in her hair with music blasting from the speakers so loud that it drowned her voice as she sang along. There was nothing but miles of open road in every direction, almost never ending, and the sun was out, warming her skin. She had never felt so free as she drove into the city limits of Amarillo. Reaching downtown, she noticed dark, heavy clouds off to the west and closing in, she turned down the radio, able to hear a loud rumble of thunder in the distance. She pulled off to get gas and was thinking this storm is gonna be a doozy as she got back into her car, keeping a watchful eye on the sky. A strong breeze carried a whiff of rain as the building clouds shadowed the desert around her. She figured she'd wait out the storm at a little coffee shop just on the edge of town. The folded-up umbrellas at the patio tables were close to lift off, with the wind picking up and metal wind chimes hanging on the neighboring shop tinging loudly. Tumbleweeds rolled across the dirt, tumbling quickly with the force of the wind, when the sky suddenly turned an alarming green hue. She put the top up on the convertible, knowing the darkening clouds were about to cut loose. As she hustled up to the coffee shop doors, purse under her arm, small hailstones began pelting her skin and the town siren screamed loudly. She pulled the door open and it whipped from her hand, slamming back against the building as employees ran for the back. Her hair flew everywhere and across her face as she entered the coffee shop. Chaos broke out as the roaring wind became louder than the shouting and what surely sounded like a dog barking. She barely got inside the door before she saw a tornado form from the sky, lowering to the desert floor maybe a few miles away. She froze for a moment, staring in amazement at the natural disaster hurling earth into the air, moving only when her arm was grabbed from behind her and the power went out with the crackling of the transformer blowing, throwing sparks like fireworks. A man pulled her by the arm, heading to the back in a rush, and just in time as a green patio umbrella flew through the storefront like a javelin, peppering the walls, floor, and tables with shards of shattered glass. His timing was impeccable as he darted into the small storage room, pulling her in and shutting the door. She could barely hear the dog whine in that dark storage room over the freight train sound, the cacophony growing louder by the second. She crouched down in a corner and covered her head with her arms. Shelves started to rattle and a few items fell to the floor. The dog lay on her feet and the man covered her body with his. She grasped his arm with one hand and held on tightly as he shielded her. She was trembling, shaking like a leaf, hoping it wasn't noticeable through the chaos of everything surrounding them, including the rattling shelves, but his voice cut through the commotion as he shouted, his voice calm and confident, "It'll be all over soon."

She recognized that voice...that smooth tone...the dog...could it be? His scent was euphoric; a familiar comfort. The outside roaring began to quiet, and mere moments later, there was an eerie silence. The dog moved from her feet and the man crouched in front of her, holding on to her upper arms.

"Are you okay?"

She just stared at him, unable to clearly make out his face, for it was still too dark in that small room. He reached back and opened the door.

"Yeah, I think I'm okay, thanks to you," she said as just enough light shined in to illuminate the mess all around them.

"Tripp?"

"We meet again," he said with a smile. She was surprised, he should've been much farther along if he was traveling Route 66 as well.

"You've come to my rescue again," she said as he stood. Taking her by the hand, he pulled her up to her feet.

"I'm sure coincidence played a part."

Her face sprouted a vulnerable smile but she was feeling a lump forming in her throat.

"Thank you for pulling me from the windows." She wrapped her arms around his neck, hugging him tightly.

"You've never seen a twister before, I'm guessing."

She shook her head no and he held her for a minute before leaning back and holding her face in his hands. Her vulnerable eyes met his and he asked, "Are you okay, really?"

"I'm not hurt."

He tucked her hair behind her shoulder then tipped her chin up.

"I know you were scared."

"Terrified, actually. You made me feel safer though." She grasped his forearms, not wanting him to let go of her.

"Good." His brown eyes peered through hanging curled strands, disheveled from the harrowing experience they survived together.

"You didn't give me a chance to dial your phone number," she said, straight face and wide eyes looking up at him.

He let out a quick chuckle in response. "Sorry about that. I'm curious to know...would you have?"

She swallowed hard and nodded. There was a pause as they

looked into each other's eyes. Perhaps it was surviving a natural disaster in the same room together, or maybe it was the fact that he kept turning up at times she needed help, but there was a connection there; a strong one. Her heart raced in her chest as they inched closer. And closer. It seemed as though their fates were intertwined.

"Everyone okay?" a barista asked in a panic as she stopped in the doorway. The two of them let go of each other and the dog ran out of the room.

"We're good, thanks," he answered, breaking the tension that had been building between them. The barista continued to the front of the coffee shop, the sound of broken glass being swept across the floor snapping them back into reality. He let out a sigh and asked, "Well, should we assess the damage?"

She nodded and followed him out of the storage room. The dog's metal tag jingled as he trotted around the shattered glass mess in the coffee shop. A warm summer breeze swept through, whisking her hair across her face as sun rays broke through the quickly dissipating clouds and danced across her skin. The sparse desert landscape was illuminated in such a way as to summon images of pioneer wagons heading west to a brighter future. Aria darted out the front door and stopped, frozen in her tracks, looking at an empty parking space where her car had been parked. Tripp came out and stood beside her, the dog following.

"I parked right here," she said, pointing.

Tripp looked around, adjusting his cap.

"You have full coverage?"

"Yeah, but where the hell is my car?" She walked in one direction as he walked in the opposite, around the backside of the shop.

"Um, I found it."

She ran to where he stood at the corner of the building and her hands flew to her face.

"Oh my God, no!"

"If it makes you feel any better, my Jeep slid three spots over and I didn't back in." He shrugged, trying to make light of the fact that her car was upside down at the edge of the property. She looked at him, eyes huge and getting misty. He stepped to her, wrapping his arms around her once again. She buried her face in his chest, unable to hold back tears. His fingers stroked her hair, his scruffy chin rested on top of her head.

"I'm so sorry, Aria."

"That car was my baby. I don't know what I'm going to do. My whole road trip is—" She sniffled and shook her head.

"You'll need to call your insurance company, but if I can be honest, it's more important that you're okay than the car."

Wet, batting eyes looked up at him. Her trembling flesh was calmed by his soft touch as he laid a hand on her back, stepping closer to her.

"I know. I know the car is just a thing but...I love that car. My luggage bag was in it too." She began to weep as she leaned her forehead against his chest again. He welcomed her emotional release, supporting her with a quiet hug before asking, "Should we go look for your bag?"

With a nod, a sniffle, and a wipe of her face, she let him lead her by the hand. Approaching the car, he bent over looking through the ripped canvas topper.

"I see it!" She stepped closer, slinging her purse strap up higher onto her shoulder, but he stopped her.

"There's broken glass everywhere. I'll get it." He knelt onto one knee and reached in, pulled the bag out, and shook glass off of it.

"Was that all you needed?"

"Yeah. Thank you."

As he handed it to her, glass crunching beneath his sneakers, he nodded and said, "I should probably go check mine out."

She walked over with him, dragging her luggage bag along on the one in-tact wheel, and watched helplessly as he walked around the Jeep, the dog following on his heels.

"Besides a few scratches, it looks okay."

"Yeah, you got lucky." She inspected the opposite side then spared another glance over her shoulder at her upside-down pride and joy.

"They jinxed it," she said to herself as he came around and stood next to her.

"What do you mean?" he asked, squatting down to pet the dog. She turned to him and said, "The girls. They asked if my car could handle the road trip. I assured them it could. Then the whole twister joke." Sadness gloomed her pretty face.

"The tire though...that could've happened to any vehicle. And this..." He stood, gesturing all around them. "This was a natural disaster. It wasn't your car being unreliable. Mustangs have a lightweight body design. I have no idea how this Jeep is right-side up, or even still in this parking lot." He tousled his dark curls and flopped his hat back on. "You did have a sweet car though. I'm sorry."

"Thanks." She turned away, fighting the urge to burst out in tears.

"Maybe this trip was a mistake. This isn't how I expected my vacation to play out."

"Sometimes heading in a direction that you think is wrong at first because it isn't familiar or easy ends up being the right direction. Lands ya right where you're supposed to be." His words were comforting.

"Free coffee in here, folks!" a barista hollered from the cracked glass door.

"I better make that phone call," she said.

"I'll get us coffee while you do that." He offered her a supportive grin and began heading back to the coffee shop.

"You plan to hang around?" she asked, taking her phone from her back pocket. He turned around and said, "Well, I'm not going to just leave you here like this."

She cracked a smile as he patted his leg for the dog to follow him into the shop. Aria couldn't help but glance in at Tripp a few times as she paced outside the window on the phone. He took two cups of hot black coffee over to a table that had managed to remain upright then tipped up two chairs and brushed them off. The glass mess had been swept up for the most part during their time outside so the dog lay at Tripp's feet, calmer, but still panting.

After giving all her information to the insurance company, Aria grabbed her luggage bag and hauled it to the door. Tripp opened it for her and brought her luggage in, propping it against the wall before sitting at the table with Aria.

"Thanks. Coffee is still hot, huh?" She blew on it before sipping it.

"Yep. Luckily, they had brewed a fresh pot right before the storm hit and the coffee pot survived."

"Good, because it's gonna be a long day."

"They let you file a claim?"

"Yeah. I need to text them photos, but even then, they're saying my policy won't cover a rental car. Total bullshit. I know I have that included. My regular agent is on vacation and the one I just spoke with is clueless. Hope his vacation is going better than mine."

"Damn. I'm sorry." He could see sentimental emotions swirling in her misty eyes, making him want to pull her onto his lap for a hug big enough to take it all away.

"I'll have to cut my trip short now. It's been a catastrophe." She rested her forehead in her hands with her elbows on the table, defeated in the attempt to take a stress-free vacation.

"So, what did you have planned for the rest of your vacation?"

"As in places to visit?" She looked up.

"Yeah. You said the other day that you had a route planned out." His eyes were connected with hers as he sipped his steaming coffee.

"Well, I planned to continue on Route 66 clear to Flagstaff then make the loop down around Phoenix and straight back to the Pensacola area."

"Well...I happen to be taking the same route and I know some great places to stop." He sipped his coffee, eyes on her.

"You're really taking the same route?" She was reluctant to believe him.

He nodded, confirming.

"I appreciate the guided tour offer but paying for a rental for that long and with that many miles would be way too expensive."

"Well, I wasn't just offering a tour."

Her head tilted and her brows wrinkled.

"It gets lonely sometimes on the road, even with Atlas."

"Atlas?"

"That's my dog's name."

"Oh!"

"What do ya say?"

"About his name? I like it. It fits being a traveler."

He chuckled. "No, I meant about traveling with us."

"Oh! Right." She looked down at the dog, who perked his ears when he looked up at her.

"You'd be okay with me tagging along?"

"If not, I wouldn't have offered. Plus, I could use a navigator."

"But I don't want you going out of your way."

"It's really not." His wink and smirk were too irresistible to refuse his offer. This was her chance, possibly the only opportunity she would ever have to get to know this guy. At best, she'd have a chance to get to know this guy better, maybe seeing him again in the future even. At worst, she'd end up in a ditch somewhere, turkey vultures feasting away at her sun-dried flesh. Either way, she'd be able to feast her eyes on this handsome stranger for a stretch and it would be the most excitement and action she'd had in forever.

"I'm just going to drag you down, Tripp."

"What? No, Aria, you're not. Really. Don't be silly."

"If you're sure, I'll take you up on your offer." She smiled, not too excitedly, for she couldn't let him see how excited she *really* was.

"It's settled then. Let's hit the road."

Windows were down in the Jeep, the radio was turned down low, and Atlas's nose was taking in fresh air with each pant, making everything feel better.

"So, I'm guessing you chose his name?" she asked, continuously chasing her hair from her face with her fingers.

"I did. I adopted him almost two years ago as a pup at a local shelter. His mom had just been hit and killed by a vehicle. I stopped and took them both to the vet. We checked for chips and injuries on this guy, but neither had a chip and I couldn't just leave him behind. I took him home that day and he's been my traveling buddy since."

"Wow, poor guy." She scratched between the dog's ears as he leaned in between the seats.

"Well, he's a lucky dog now. He seems happy."

"Yeah, he might be spoiled."

"That's not a bad thing."

"Steaks are his favorite treat too, so yeah, very spoiled." Tripp bumped his elbow into her arm and chuckled before patting the dog's head that popped up between theirs. "We'll stop at a good place for a bite before leaving town."

"Sounds good. So, you mentioned you're on a trip for work. What exactly is your job title? It seems like you have a pretty cool job," Aria asked, petting the dog but avoiding the drool about to get on her hand.

"Yeah, I do. I got lucky. So, my title is travel content coordinator. I travel and blog about different destinations. I write articles for a magazine called *Tails & Trails*. It's mainly a Western magazine but we feature all areas of the country with travel articles in each issue. I travel sometimes up to a month at a time then work remotely to put it all together for submission. We had a photographer until recently, so for now, I'm the photographer too."

"Sounds like a blast."

"It is, yeah. I love it. I actually liked my last job too, so I always make sure to incorporate an article corresponding to that in each issue of the magazine."

"Okay, so inquiring minds need to know...what was your last job?" She adjusted her sunglasses on top of her head.

"I was a wilderness survival instructor. I taught at military boot camps and prisons."

"Prisons? Wow, that's cool."

"Yeah. It felt like I was doing some good, ya know? Like, helping the inmates find a good moral path. It was nice to see most of them really take an interest. It was a bit challenging to teach what I needed to teach without being able to use anything that could be considered a weapon though." He shrugged with a chuckle.

"That's what PowerPoint is for." Aria knocked elbows with him.

"Exactly."

"So how did you end up switching careers?"

"Well, funding was redistributed and my program was cut."

"I bet the inmates weren't happy about that."

"No, they weren't. That course was taught to the good-behavior inmates that were trying to stay on a clean path so it gave them something to look forward to each week. I told them that our minds can act as a compass, you know. We tend to go where our minds take us. They need to make sure it's in a direction worth living. I still write to each of them when I get time."

"I'm sure they appreciate that. That's great advice. Sounds like they respected you."

He nodded with a crooked smile but still had a saddened twinkle in his eyes.

"Well, maybe in your downtime you could take those lessons that you would've taught in class and create weekly videos. I know you wouldn't be getting paid for it, but if you think they would be able to view them somehow...maybe during library hours?"

His brows raised and he turned to her. "That's actually a brilliant idea. I'm sure I could find a way to reach them with the info.

The military decided to use resources and instructors from within so they're not in need. The correctional facilities and prisons though, that idea could work."

"You could post the videos online and gain subscribers."

"That's a great idea. I think I'll do that when my travels are done this month. Thanks for the idea."

"Sure. I'm sorry about funding being cut. Sounds like that job was important to you."

"It was, thanks. Luckily, the job I have now allows me to make use of bits and pieces of the lessons. Jake, my boss, is great. He's the magazine's travel advertising manager."

"A job is so much more enjoyable when you have a cool boss. I dabbled a bit in photography when I was in college." She leaned back comfortably in the passenger seat, his camera bag on her lap.

"Oh yeah? Ya any good?"

"Yeah, I had to choose an elective so I picked that and enjoyed it. I wasn't horrible at it."

"Still use that knowledge?"

"I mean, I take photos for fun, but I'm sure technology has changed enough since college that I wouldn't know what I'm doing now."

He laughed as she checked out the functions on his camera.

"Whoever hired you for this job knew what they were doing," she added.

"Yeah? What makes you say that?"

She was flipping through photos he had taken on the camera.

"Because these photos are great. Hope you don't mind me being nosey."

"I don't mind and thanks. I'm sure an actual photographer could do better."

"Don't sell yourself short, Tripp. These aren't rookie quality."

"I appreciate that. Maybe you should give it a whirl." He flashed a white smile her way, making her blush.

She looked at him and shook her head no.

"Why not?" he asked sincerely.

"I don't wanna be responsible for that." She giggled and put the camera back in the camera bag.

"Well, I'm sure they'd turn out just fine, so if you get the urge to play around with the camera, go for it."

She nodded, low self-confidence showing in the polite smile she flashed his way. Her stare concentrated out the window a few minutes before he broke the silence with a question.

"So, what do *you* do for work?"

"I'm a pediatric nurse at a specialty children's hospital. It's mainly cancer patients."

"Oh, wow. I bet that's a tough job. Very honorable though."

"Thanks. I'm burned out, to be honest. The long hours, the sadness...it's beginning to take its toll on me."

"I can imagine. Wow, that must be stressful. I bet it's an amazing feeling when a case turns out positive though."

"It is. Especially since it doesn't happen often. It's definitely an emotional rollercoaster when one of them pulls through. Some of those kids are our patients for so long that we become close to them, even though we aren't supposed to."

"I'm sure it's difficult not to."

"It is. Ya get to know these kids well when ya see them every single day. Their families too. Maybe I just get attached too easily."

"That's not a bad thing."

"No?"

"No."

"I know this is why nurses are told not to get attached to patients when we are hired in. We're reminded daily to not get attached, to just do our job and go home, but it doesn't work that way, at least not with me. I've tried."

"Again, it's not a bad thing. It proves you're a big-hearted person."

"Or sensitive."

"Not a bad thing either."

There was that warm smile again. Something, everything,

about this guy was comforting. She had a strong instinct about people and there were no red flags with Tripp.

"Thank you for saying that," she said, her chin tipped downward as she tucked her flyaway hair behind her ear.

"I just call it as I see it."

The heat in her cheeks revved up again.

"You seem like a good guy."

"I appreciate that. I try."

"I just call it as I see it." Her smile reflected in the windshield.

"Do you have or want kids of your own?" he asked. "Sorry, if that's too personal, you don't have to—"

"I've never been in a relationship worthy of wanting children from it. I feel like...I don't know...like I have given up on both."

"Still?" he asked, his brow turning down, worried he may become disappointed really quickly.

She smiled. "I don't want to have children."

He nodded, pretending to understand so she wouldn't feel the need to further explain.

"I sound like a horrible person, don't I?"

"What? No, not at all. Millions of people choose not to have children. If everyone in the world had them, the world would be way more over-populated than it is."

"True."

"I um...I actually *can't* have children."

She turned more toward him with curiosity in her eyes. "*Can't?*"

"Yeah." He looked over at her, noting the furrow to her brow and the sad, downturned tick to her lips that are usually so quick to smile. "It's okay. I'm okay with it. It's probably meant to be with my job and all."

"I'm sorry, Tripp. I didn't mean to—"

"No, no, it's okay. Really." He rubbed her arm, static sparking on her skin with his touch and causing him to jerk his hand back quickly; a reflex. It was as if he had shuffled across carpet in slippers during the dry-air winter. "I guess there's still static in the air. Sorry about that."

"It's okay. I've always been sensitive to static. It's the high magnetism in my body."

"That sounds interesting. Remind me to not let you pump gas."

He sparked a laugh in her.

Mile Marker 5: Steaks & Cadillacs

Tripp held the door open for Aria as they entered the steak house. He looked so good in that green-pocketed button-up short-sleeved shirt and jeans. It was a fresh look; like dew on early morning grass

"This place has the best Texan Steaks. Not just here in Amarillo, I mean anywhere in Texas that I've tried."

"I take it you've tried many places?" Aria asked as they followed the hostess to a two-top cocktail table near the outdoor bar.

"I have. Texas is known for steaks, so when in Rome, right?" He chuckled.

"Sure. Steak does sound good," she agreed as she took the stool Tripp pulled out for her.

"It's nice they have an outdoor bar so Atlas can join."

"Absolutely. He'd much rather eat his steak here than in the Jeep. He'd be jealous." Tripp looped Atlas's leash around the bottom of his stool leg before taking his seat and they wasted no time in ordering.

"Do you object to me ordering a beer?"

She giggled. "No, why would I?" She adjusted the long-sleeved shirt she had tied around her waist in case the temperature plummeted, reconsidering the white tank top tucked into her jean shorts and her white canvas shoes she had worn to top off her casual look.

"Well, I'm driving. Although, I suppose you could if I needed you to."

"I'm sure you'll be okay to drive after just one or two."

"Okay. You ordering a drink?" he asked as he nodded at the bartender.

"Maybe just one. I'm a lightweight. I don't drink often."

"Neither do I but I like one with a steak."

The sun was sinking, just an orange glow left on the western horizon and the multicolored lights in the shape of cacti strung over the bar seemed to grow brighter with each passing second as the darkness deepened.

As the bartender set their drinks on the bar in front of them and took their food order, the small stage across the patio came to life and country music poured from the speakers, the rhythm bringing Aria's body to life. She grabbed her drink and started walking backward toward the small dance floor, a flirty smile spreading across her face and that 'dance with me' look filling her eyes. "Don't tell me you're not much of a dancer, either..."

Atlas remained completely unbothered, too focused on begging the neighboring patrons to share their meals with him.

"Get on out here." She waved for him to join her as she stepped out onto the dirt dance floor among other people and put that brown bottle to her lips. The look he shot her was intense. It was as though he was shy and about to break eye contact but couldn't because she was breathtaking. He watched her dance a moment, standing and leaning against the table. She had not a care in the world. His smile was uncontrollable when she twirled around, hair flying outward like a windmill spinning in the wind, sweeping behind her as she pivoted 180 degrees. He was admiring her carefree spirit and feminine beauty. She waved at him again, impatiently this time, but with a laugh.

"Stay," he told Atlas before joining Aria within the growing crowd. He had just started to loosen up and show off a few moves when the music switched gears into a song meant for slow dancing. She tipped back her beer then said, "Come on, you came for steak." Before she could take a few steps toward the table, he grabbed the shirt she had tied around her waist and pulled her to him. Surprised, she stumbled as she turned to him and he caught her with an arm around the small of her back. She managed to not spill her beer but realized she was steadying herself with a hand on his chest. He didn't seem to mind as he gazed into her green eyes and took her hand up in the air above their heads for a twirl. She whirled smack into his chest. They laughed as she gripped his shoulder to steady herself, dirt shuffling beneath her feet.

"Ya know, I'm a pretty lucky guy."

"Oh? Why's that?"

"Not only am I the guy you asked to dance with you, but you'll be leaving here with me tonight."

She giggled out of pure delight over those words.

"I'm flattered. That also makes me a pretty lucky lady." She quickly realized sleeping arrangements had not yet been discussed, but figured she'd go with the flow instead of bringing it up at that moment.

He led a slow dance, holding her close. No words were spoken, just a smile and a twirl before he pulled her back to him once again. She made his heart skip a beat just as he did hers. Swaying together, they were the last remaining couple out on that dirt. Their steps only stopped when the music did, still in a world of all their own, and their bodies leaned in to fill the barely-there gap between them. He looked as though he wanted his parting lips to connect with hers, when—

"Order up!" the bartender shouted, ringing a dinner triangle, and Atlas let out a loud bark. Distracted, Tripp chuckled, flashing those pearly whites, and dropped his head, disappointed in missing the chance. She smiled, excited that he was showing interest, and took his hand, leading him back to the table. Atlas had already finished his steak, licking the plate on the ground before

Aria and Tripp began eating theirs. They spent the evening lying on their backs on the hood of the Jeep, kicked back watching airplane traffic light up the sky in Amarillo. Low-flying planes zoomed by, blowing their hair around and making them laugh. Gas station popcorn didn't disappoint as they shared a bag in the dark, parked just outside of street light glare, stars dancing on the windshield behind them.

∼

At nine the next morning, Tripp was loading up the Jeep outside of a sleepy motel a ways outside of Amarillo. Aria rolled her lopsided luggage bag out to the Jeep and greeted Atlas with a friendly head scratch.

"You sleep okay?" Tripp asked as he put her bag in the back.

"I did, thanks. You?" She couldn't help but notice how his athletic build was evident through the snug V-neck t-shirt and black joggers he wore.

"Not bad. The rooms are pretty clean for a hole-in-the-wall place." His swallowing was constricted. She wore a floral print romper, almost short enough for her ass cheeks to show when she walked, with thin straps revealing the smooth curve of her shoulders. His temperature was rising quickly, considering how early in the morning it was still.

"Yeah, mine was clean too."

"The coffee in my room was horrible though." He shut the back door of the Jeep with a *thud*.

"I didn't take time to try it. We can stop somewhere for some if you want."

"Sure. Hold the tornados though." His dry humor struck again. The sound of her laughter tingled down his spine as he opened her door for her. She couldn't help but find the gesture chivalrous.

After stopping for breakfast, Tripp asked, "Feel like being adventurous?"

"Always. What do ya have in mind?"

He looked over at her with a grin.

"You're surprising me, aren't you?"

"Yep. We're gonna dust off the cobwebs and get you out there into the world. I'm gonna show you what you've been missing."

A little way up the road, he pulled off into what looked like a colorful junkyard; an organized one, but a junkyard nonetheless. Her brows wrinkled as he jumped out and opened her door, Atlas jumping out behind her.

"We aren't stealing anything, are we?" she asked as they entered a metal gate.

"What? No! No, not at all." He laughed, tucking a water bottle under his arm.

"You've been here before?" she asked as they approached a little building with a side window. Tripp slipped cash under the window slit and nodded for Aria to follow, Atlas on his heels.

"Grab a few," he instructed as he grabbed a few spray cans of colored paint.

"The sign said this is a ranch." Aria was completely confused as she didn't pay attention to the whole sign when they drove by it.

"Yep. This is a Cadillac Ranch."

"As in cars, obviously," she said as they rounded a corner and came to a long row of old Cadillacs with graffiti painted on them. Tripp started shaking cans so she followed suit.

"This is pretty cool." She began spraying her name.

"Yeah, it is. Creative. I don't know who came up with the idea but it's pretty popular around here." He sprayed his name near hers, both of them careful to not get paint on their clothes. Tripp poured water from the water bottle onto the bottom of Atlas's right paw and pressed it into the dirt to make a muddy paw print under their names. Atlas ran off to chase tumbleweeds and looked to be regretting grabbing hold of one with his teeth. He rolled around, dirt clouding all around him.

"Atlas! Ugh he's gonna be a mess." Tripp shook his head in

disappointment as he cleaned his sunglasses with the bottom of his shirt.

"Oh, he already is. Your Jeep will be a mess too." She giggled as she outlined her name with a different color.

"We should add something that represents this trip," she suggested.

"Hmm..." He pondered a moment before it came to him. He grabbed the can of gray paint and sprayed a tornado between their names.

"Perfect." She laughed, spraying an outline of a coffee mug in black at the base of the tornado then filled the top line with brown, but as if it were splashing from the tilted cup.

"Now it's perfect," he agreed, his paint-stained hands in his pockets as he stood back to take a look before adding a bright green cactus. Not to be outdone, she added a cute cartoon outline of Atlas around the paw print. They both used their phones to snap a photo of their collaborated masterpiece then she asked him to take a group photo. He snapped a lid back onto a can and tossed it to the ground, sliding his phone in his pocket as she set hers up on a set of pallets and set the timer. She ran back and stood next to him in front of their graffiti art, his arm around her shoulders. They had fun with a few poses, and when she posted them to social media as they drove out of the gate and onto the asphalt, she titled the post: "A whirlwind of fun. What a Tripp it's been so far!"

Mile Marker 6: Rainstorm

Atlas insisted a pit stop be made out in the middle of nowhere. The scenic view along Route 66 was too incredible to pass up photographing. While Atlas did his business and took advantage of the space to stretch his legs, Aria and Tripp decided to as well. She rounded the front of the Jeep and reached back in on the driver's side next to Tripp to turn up the radio, as he had just stepped out and was still holding the door open. In the middle of the road, she whirled around in her flaring ruffled country skirt like a tumbleweed blowing gracefully across the open plains, stirring up a storm of passion within him. He couldn't take his eyes off her. She seemed innocent and oblivious as to how her every move was making his blood rush south from his quickly beating heart. She turned to see him leaning against the Jeep admiring her and stood a moment, admiring him and the way he looked at her. That sensual smile of his warmed her heart. His hair was plastered to his forehead, sweat already gathering under the edge of his baseball cap. Using the bottom of his shirt to wipe sweat off his face, those abs and that faint love trail downward disappeared under the front of his jeans. Oh, the tease! She gasped and turned around but he saw her staring and shied away with a dazzling smile. She was beginning to sweat from every pore of her body as well, secretly sniffing her armpits when he turned to look for Atlas, who hadn't wandered far. It didn't matter how much of a mess they were; he was sexy and she was just as radiant. One of the straps on her tank top fell off her shoulder as he went to snap a photo of her on his phone. She was about to lift it, a finger underneath, when he said with a hand out, "Wait! Leave it!" She left it hanging low, and when she playfully touched her chin to her shoulder, as if she were about to turn away, and smiled a coy smile, he snapped a perfect shot. A loud roar of thunder rolled overhead as a bolt of lightning struck the ground out in the plains. It was louder than the music that still blared from the Jeep speakers. Sudden rainfall surprised them, coming down hard and fast.

"What the hell? Where did that come from?" Aria hollered as she ran toward him. He met her at the back of the Jeep.

"I didn't even notice a dark cloud in the sky," he hollered over another crack of thunder as he scooped her up in his arms, spinning her around with his grasp below her rear. She laughed, holding her sunhat on her head with one hand and gripping his shoulder with the other. They were soaking wet without a care in the world. The rain quickly extinguished the heat between them, soaking them both, and Atlas barked as he jumped into the Jeep. Her form began showing through her wet clothes as they clung to her skin and he was starting to overheat all over again. Atlas barked again, apparently attempting to save them from the storm they were enjoying, so Tripp let Aria down, sliding her down his chest so she was still close to him. Upon getting back into the Jeep, doors closed and the rain quieter, she turned down the radio as he stretched his arm into the backseat, trying to reach his bag of clothes. Hers was all the way in the back, unreachable.

"I can reach it," Aria said as she turned backward, leaning to pull the zipper open on his bag. It was obvious she was wearing a thong under that ruffled skirt when she was bent over and he turned, quickly facing forward. He exhaled a slow long breath, raking his hair back, pretending he saw nothing.

"Just a t-shirt is good if you can grab one, please. One for you too if you want," he said before clearing his throat.

"Here." She tossed one into his lap, surprising him before sitting back into her seat holding one for herself, her wet hair having flopped against his shoulder.

"Thanks." He peeled his wet gray t-shirt off over his head, those flexing back muscles and triceps having her full attention, and tossed it onto the floor in the back. She was blatantly staring at him, practically drooling, taking careful note of how the fabric of the fresh, dry, white V-neck t-shirt he pulled down over his torso wrinkled at the front of his shoulders. His perfectly toned physique...those muscles looked amazing with that shirt hugging every curve of his sculpted shoulders and biceps. The hint of chest showing at the deep collar drove her crazy, sweat and rain glistening in the gray light. Averting her eyes to the window and clearing her throat, she fought the urge to ask him to quench her thirst. Realizing she hadn't yet changed, she told him, "Oh, I can change while you drive." He nodded and the tires flung mug as they pulled off the shoulder and back onto pavement. She tossed her hat into the back seat and, conserving her modesty the best she could, turned her back to him to remove her drenched tank top, putting the t-shirt on right away. Her hair blocked his view of any side-breast action and he kept trying to look away out of respect and keep his attention on the road. She wasn't that modest but didn't want to be too *free* around him yet either. She stripped her skirt off then pulled the t-shirt down as far as it would go to cover her panties. He rubbed his sweaty, clammy palm repeatedly across the thigh of his jeans and she loved the way it seemed to be torturing him. Keeping her legs together, pulled up in the seat, she sat facing more toward him.

"If you don't mind me saying...that's a good look on you...in my shirt," he said quietly, then cleared his throat, not able to look at her.

"You glad you wore jeans instead of joggers?" she asked as he took a drink of water and almost spit it out all over the steering wheel.

Mile Marker 7: UTE Lake & No Mistakes

"So where to next?" Aria asked, her tanned toes tapping the dash, warm sun rays striping her ankles and sunglow accentuating her cheekbones and those few freckles on the top of her nose which drew his attention, and with a smile, asked, "Did you have anywhere in mind?"

"Not really. Just sightseeing," she said as she applied tinted Chapstick from her purse to her lips, smacking them together. The simple gesture made him pull in his bottom lip, sucking on it for a moment. Pulling down the visor mirror, she checked for sloppy imperfections, smudging her middle finger tip across her top lip.

"Okay. Logan then."

"What's in Logan?"

"Ute Lake State Park."

"Let's do it."

"I like that you're easy going."

"Yeah?"

"Yeah. Wanna grab lunch on the way and we'll take it into the park? There should be picnic tables."

"Sounds perfect."

They grabbed subs at a sandwich shop along the way. One for

Atlas too, of course. Tripp put Atlas on the leash, not wanting him to run off at the park, but also out of respect for other park visitors. The area was pretty flat, brown being the color taking over the scenery with the dry desert clay.

"The water looks refreshing," Aria observed before taking a bite.

"Sure does. I think Atlas is thinking the same thing." He nodded at the dog, who had already devoured his meat-filled sub and had his ears perked, looking in the direction of the water and sniffing the fresh air.

"You pack a suit?"

"Really? We gonna swim?" she asked excitedly.

"Why not? It's hot as Hell out here."

She giggled and nodded. "I did bring a couple. Did you?"

"Always."

"You practically live in that Jeep, don't you?" she says, her head tipped to the side, questioning but envying him.

"Pretty much. I don't know why I even have a house. I'm always on the job it seems like. Do you like your job?" He crumpled up his sandwich wrapper and placed it back into the bag.

"I don't know anymore. I like parts of it, but it can be so depressing."

"How long have you been a nurse?"

"Six years, but it feels like it's been so much longer. I thought that I'd be saving lives every day going into that field."

"I'm sure you do."

She smiled. "I appreciate that. Some days I guess I do, or at least keep the patients alive. I wish there weren't sad days. I wish I could save them all. I thought that since I don't have kids of my own, this particular job may be easier for me than many other nurses. I was wrong."

"I can imagine it would be harder though for them."

"And I can't imagine what that's like for them to come home and hug their kids so tightly, hoping and praying they'll never have to endure what our precious patients go through."

"No kid should have to go through that. It takes one hell of a person to treat those patients and live with that every day. You should be proud of yourself. The kids who do recover...they do so because of you and nurses like you." He took her empty wrapper and took the trash over to a nearby trash can.

"Thank you." She swished her hair from her face as he walked back to the table.

"For what?"

"For what you said. Thank you."

"Of course." He unwrapped Atlas's leash from the leg of the picnic table. "Wanna hike first, then cool off?"

"Sounds good." She got up from the table and walked along next to him on a marked trail.

"I know nursing school has cost you a lot of time and money, but if it's not something you see yourself doing long-term, have you given thought to changing careers?"

"Lately, yes. It's been costing me sleep and tears. I feel like I've made a moral commitment though, if that makes sense."

"You wouldn't be a horrible person if you chose a different path."

"No?"

"No, absolutely not."

"Does it make me weak?"

"What? No!"

"I'd feel like a coward."

"What are you talking about?" He stopped walking at the edge of a shallow bluff and faced her.

"It's not like those kids can just say 'time-out, cancer, I don't wanna do this anymore.'"

"I get that but—" He suddenly turned her by her shoulders to face the water. "You see that?"

"The water?"

"All of it. The water; the way it ripples when those boats glide through it. These bluffs, this dirt, the fresh air and the blue sky, the clouds rolling overhead making us feel so small in this huge world...all of it."

She closed her eyes and took a deep breath, then opened them and looked at him.

"Can you imagine the number of kids, people in general, that you've helped live to be able to take in the everyday? You've given the chance to keep living to so many people. Kids, definitely, but also the parents of those kids who may not have had a will to carry on if the worst would've happened to their child. You've made life enjoyable again for others. For the ones less fortunate, you filled their last days with love and care and support. Hell, I'm proud of you! There's nothing more noble than that."

She swallowed the lump in her throat and said, "I appreciate your candor, every word you just said, I do. I feel I have a responsibility to those who I haven't even met yet though."

He gently took her face in his hands and his forehead met hers, his touch slightly shaky as he fought to maintain control of his nerve. He suddenly seemed more comfortable, less of a prickly cactus with touch. "You have a responsibility to yourself too. Your life and your happiness matter, so whatever career path you choose, you owe it to yourself to be happy, especially after having put others before yourself for so long."

"Maybe so. I feel like I'm chasing something that's faster than me, always just out of my reach."

"Well, it can't be love because ya don't chase that. If and when you're aligned with the stars, love will gravitate toward you. So it must be a purpose, right? I think your job serves a purpose, but if you still feel you're missing something, you'll have to go searching or be patient and let whatever it is find you."

She stared into his espresso eyes, hands flat against his back and her eyes becoming glassy as she felt the lump in her throat returning, large enough to suffocate her. Her hair crossed in front of her face with a breeze, but when that breeze died down a moment, his lips met hers, softly but passionately. That throat lump dissipated and she was now concentrating on this man in front of her who she had quickly grown so fond of. She had no idea that he had been evaluating his chances with her. For how long, she wasn't sure. Pressing her hands to his chiseled chest, she resisted the urge to let her hands wander. His dark stubble that so perfectly traced his jawline tickled her chin. A tingle ran through her body, an excitement that she hadn't felt in so long. Hearts pounded and pulses raced as she pulled her lips from his, palm still against him as she pulled away. The look in her eyes was heated but he had a confused knot in his stomach.

"I'm sorry," he quickly apologized.

"No, don't be. You have nothing to apologize for."

His tousled curls hung in front of his brow and he ran his fingers through them from front to back, relieving his sight of the obstruction, then quickly looked away from her. "I should've asked—"

"No. You were a complete gentleman. In fact, I liked the surprise. I just...I'm sorry for being so emotional. You're so sweet."

"But?" Searching for a clue, his eyes squinting against the sunlight with his head tilted to the side and a brow arched.

"No! No buts! I don't know why I pulled away."

"Too soon?"

"No, it was perfect."

"I didn't kiss you out of pity, just so you know."

She sighed with relief.

"Did you think that I had?"

"I don't know. I was hoping not."

Holding on to her waist, he looked into her eyes and said, "I sincerely wanted to kiss you. I've wanted to since we were in that storage room. When the chaos settled, I wanted to put you up against the wall but I didn't want you to assume it was due to the near-death experience. And it's not like we had spent time together, not like we have the last few days. This road trip would've been quite boring without you. I'm enjoying this, all of it."

"Me too. Maybe things happened the way they did for a reason."

"I don't actually believe in coincidences." He brushed her hair from her face.

"I'm beginning to think I don't either. I never expected to run into someone like you on this road trip, but I'm so glad I did. I came on this vacation to find myself and I found you. So far, you've helped me make this journey back to me an adventure."

"Have you found yourself though?" He fought a charming smirk.

"I'm getting there, thanks to you."

"Ya know, they say you really get to know someone when on a road trip with them, assuming that's not how ya first meet. I'm glad we met this way."

"Me too." She looked at him a moment before boldly kissing him, her lips pressed firmly to his, his brows raised with surprise. His dark curls were so soft and sprung with the twirl of her finger. Those alluring eyes of his were like a deep vortex, sucking her into oblivion, and she liked the uncertainty of where she would end up; a new dimension perhaps, one she wouldn't mind getting lost in. He felt like an instant new lease on life, a new beginning, a do-over. She wanted to start something new and have it be with him. It had to be with him; no one else could make her feel this way. Suddenly, she felt attached to and even possessive over him. What a breath of fresh air he was. Their lips tangled and his caring touch almost made her emotional again, but in a good way. Not only did he truly care, but he also made her see things in a whole different light. Her view of the path ahead was clear now. The direction her life was going in was about to veer into the unknown and instead of being scared of it, she was excited to see where this new direction would take her. Who knew this new person could have such a strong impact and so quickly? He didn't tell her what to think or how to feel, yet still made her realize she needed to make a change in order to be happy. At this moment, here with him, she actually was happy;

she was happier and felt free and more alive than she had in a long time. The pull-away was slow, made to feel even more so by the intense eye contact they maintained. She felt her cheeks heating up, not knowing what to say but savoring the moment. An approving smile spread slowly across his face. She couldn't look away from him; he was so attractive. There was an undeniable magnetic pull within the heated tension between the two of them, drawing them closer. The connection they shared felt natural to her, a sense of home.

"If you two love-birds are in search of a place to stay nearby, there's a great bed and breakfast just up the road a few miles. Great views too," an elderly gentleman passing by on the trail suggested with a smile. His wife, arm-in-arm with him, waved. Tripp gave a slow nod and a warm smile. "Thank you, much appreciated."

Aria was surprised he didn't correct the old man with the technicality of them not exactly being love birds...yet. Instead, he took hold of her hand before turning to her.

"I don't want to do this anymore," she said slowly, realization written across her face, but it wasn't obvious to him what it was she was realizing. His expression was of disappointment and he let go of her hand gracefully.

"Okay."

She grabbed his hand and smiled wide. "No, I didn't mean you, us. I meant my career. I'm going to quit."

"What?" He looked relieved yet confused, but his shoulders fell, relaxed.

"Thank you...for everything. For making me realize that I've been going about life all wrong."

"I wouldn't say you have been doing it wrong. If you wouldn't have needed a vacation so badly, we wouldn't have met."

"True. I have no regrets, but it's definitely time for a change."

"What are you going to do?"

"I don't know. But I feel lighter already."

His light touch across the side of her face was all the assurance she needed that she was making the right decision. His deliberate gesture, ever so slight but impressionable.

"Just make sure before you quit that it's really what you want to do."

She looked out over the water for a moment, then back at him.

"I'm sure. I want to travel more and not work such long hours, not be so damn stressed and have built up emotions that tear me down until I'm crying on my knees. Literally."

"Well, then I think you should quit. I'm sure you were debating the idea before your trip even began. I hope my influence doesn't make you regret this decision later."

"I was thinking it over actually. With you so far, I'm not regretting anything." The wide smile across her face was as bright as the sun shining down on them.

"You have the most beautiful smile," he told her before kissing her lips. She pulled him closer, her hands sliding down his back slowly.

"You make me smile, Tripp."

Mile Marker 8: A Desert Rose

Coming off the detoured path and rolling into Tucumcari, Aria noticed a TeePee gift shop and asked Tripp if they could stop. He was more than happy to oblige. The dry desert heat pummeled them in the face as soon as they stepped out, radiating from the Jeep and clay ground. Tripp snapped Atlas's leash on before catching up with Aria. He watched her walk in her long, country, off-the-shoulder dress, and the slit up each side in the front showed off her legs when she walked. Her tall brown boots matched the dress print perfectly. The small shop was impressive and cultural. Rows upon rows of shelving covered in trinkets and hand-made items filled the space, interrupted only by bright, vibrant paintings and heavily beaded tapestries. Tripp came up behind her and placed a necklace around her neck, latching it. She felt for it and looked down but he gently took her by the shoulders and led her to the side to face a decorative mirror. "This necklace was screaming your name. What do ya think?" he asked, looking at their reflection from behind her. The necklace was a small silver compass rose pendant with beautiful detail. Smiling, she not only loved the necklace and the way it looked on her, but how sweet it was of him to pick something so fitting out, and just for her.

"I love this."

"Yeah?"

She turned to face him, one hand on the pendant, and took his hand with the other.

"Yeah, I do."

He nodded at the cashier to ring it up.

"Did you find anything else you like?"

"I was just browsing but no, just this. You?"

"I was browsing for you. I'm good."

She reached for her purse as they approached the counter but he reached out, tapping his card before she could pull hers out.

"Tripp."

His smile began before he looked over at her.

"You didn't need to do that."

"Sure I did. That was the point."

"What was?" he asked with a nod to the clerk as they walked out of the shop.

"Putting that necklace on you that I knew you'd like, so I could buy you something. So now you have something from me; from our traveling adventure together. A compass rose for my desert rose."

"This is so sweet. It's perfect. Thank you."

He took her arm in his, a huge smile on his face, which turned out to be contagious. She stopped suddenly, felt her head, and said, "I must have set my sunglasses down inside. I'll be right back."

When she returned with her glasses on her face, he opened the passenger door to the Jeep, and before she got in, she thanked him. Pulling her to him, he kissed her; a sweet gentle kiss, one on her lips, then one on her forehead. Maybe he's trying to show her that he's falling for her as hard and fast as she is for him. Maybe she was on the exact path she was meant to be on. Her life seemed to be taking a more positive direction since meeting Tripp. He was even kind of a hero, a Hercules to her damsel in distress in more ways than one. Maybe he was what the universe had been guiding her to all along. Whether this—he—was meant to be or not, meeting him changed things for the better. How long it lasted didn't matter. She caught herself staring over at him as he drove. Those curls catching the wind and his elbow resting on the open window frame. She paid no attention to her hair constantly whipping her face because she was in awe of how he looked so free and happy. She wanted that; free and happy. She wanted him too. She had never desired anyone so badly. His gaze was captivating, whether it was purposeful or not. He glanced over at her and the smile on her face made one side of his mouth rise and his hand fell to her bare knee, patting it as if testing out new territory. He left it there when she didn't protest or move away. Atlas barked over top the console between pants so Tripp patted the pooch's head, laughing before returning his hand to the same spot on her knee. This time she took hold of it. Those curls bounced as he turned to look at her, her shy smile letting him know she was accepting of his touch. Her gaze turned to the open passenger window and her fingers gave his hand a squeeze. He couldn't contain a wide, white smile.

"Life is full of detours, unexpected winding turns, and much uncertainty, Aria."

"Some are milestones we don't forget on a path I don't regret taking." She played with the pendant, elbow on the window edge and looking down at the silver compass in her fingers. Only then did she notice it was engraved on the back. It read "Going Places". She looked over at him and he nodded his head but never took his eyes off the road as he smiled.

Mile Marker 9: Bed & Breakfast

Tripp rolled their bags into the little bed and breakfast while Aria walked Atlas in on the leash, joined him at the front desk.

"Can we get two rooms, please? Or one with two beds?" Tripp got his ID out of his wallet.

"We've only got one room left, sir. It's only got a queen-sized bed," the old man at the counter stated. Tripp dropped his head with a smile before looking over at Aria for approval and mumbling, "Of course you do."

Tongue in cheek, she asked, "Pet friendly?"

"Sure. He looks clean enough." The old man grabbed the last key hanging on the corkboard behind him and slapped it on the counter, then took Tripp's ID to make a copy.

"You okay with sharing a room?" he asked her quietly, his back and elbow against the counter.

"Sure, it's fine by me."

"I don't want you to feel uncomfortable."

"Are you going to feel uncomfortable?" she asked, chin up.

"No, I just don't want you to feel, ya know..."

"Pressured?"

He turned his head away and nodded.

"It's okay, Tripp. Really. I gained trust for you quickly. Do you snore?"

"I don't think so. Atlas hasn't complained." He chuckled.

"Here ya go." The old man handed Tripp his ID and said, "Second room to the right upstairs."

"Thank you." Tripp scooped the key off the counter and handed it to Aria so he could carry their bags up the stairs. Aria opened their room door, and as they entered, they both said, "Wow!" Tripp dropped the bags and joined her at the big floor-to-ceiling window across the room. The view was amazing; the last of the colors from the nearly set sun still painted across the sand.

"We can look at the stars from right here." Aria pointed out a few stars already shining up high in the sky.

"Think we should move the bed over here?" he asked.

"If it's not bolted down, yeah, absolutely." She loved the idea. He tossed a nod in the direction of the bed so she joined him at the headboard, one on each side of the bed. Together, they pushed the bed from the wall over to the window that comprised almost the entire wall. The foot of the bed pressed against the window lightly, just enough to close any gap.

"I feel like I need a shower." She brushed a smudge of desert clay off the side of her leg below her knee.

"Yeah, go ahead. I'll take one after you."

"You wanna go first?" She stopped, holding her bag.

"No, of course not. You go."

She nodded and disappeared with her bag into the bathroom. When she came out, she was wearing a fitted tank top and bed shorts. His attention was on her and the fact that she was braless. She pulled at the front a bit, trying to make it less obvious. His eyes shied away and he tried to fight a smile, making a show of grabbing his bag.

"Your turn. I tried to leave enough hot water for you."

"Thanks. I don't think I need it too warm tonight though." He walked past her to the bathroom, grinning ear to ear, as she didn't clue in to the point he was making, and she made herself comfortable on one side of the bed, debating on positioning a pillow in the center to separate them. Atlas came over to her side of the bed and sat, ears perked, staring at her and whining.

"You need to go outside?" she asked the dog, which started jumping around and ran for the door, so she got up and slipped her shoes on, hooked Atlas to the leash, and walked him downstairs and outside. When she returned to the room, she opened the door, Atlas pushing his way through first, and Tripp was just walking out of the bathroom, steam from the shower clouding behind him. His hair was dripping wet as he toweled it off, his shoulders and chest wet and shiny. The towel around his waist was holding on for dear life, hugging his body just beneath the top curve of his hips. She stopped dead in her tracks, Atlas about strangling himself before jerking the leash from her hand.

"I wondered where you went." He ran his fingers through his towel-dried hair.

"Atlas needed outside."

"I figured since he was missing too." He grinned, getting a pair of shorts from his bag, obviously having forgotten to take clothes into the bathroom with him.

"Smartass." She smiled, but that grin of his made her bite her lip. Well, that and the fact that he was nearly naked. She was trying not to stare, not wanting to seem impolite, but couldn't look away for long either. His physique was sizzling, mind-melting hot. She didn't notice that she had just dropped the leash as she stared, her saliva drying up with a sudden case of cottonmouth. He began walking to her and her heart pounded faster with each step he took.

"I'll take it off," he said as he approached her. She felt like ice rapidly melting on desert asphalt in the heat of a summer day as she managed to choke out, "Hmm?" followed by an exaggerated swallow. The firm curves of his upper arms looked even better with his shirt off.

"The leash." He bent down and unclipped the dog's leash

from the collar as Atlas just stood near her as if he weren't free to move about.

"Oh! Right..." She relaxed enough to feel like an idiot.

"You okay?" he asked, standing up straight, as she still had yet to move away from the door.

"Yeah." She snapped out of her trance. "It's actually chilly outside." She crossed her arms in front of her.

"It gets chilly at night in the desert. I thought about going outside for a while to look at the stars but it surprisingly got cold fast tonight. Next best thing right here." He pointed over at the bed. She didn't want to seem too eager to lay next to him so she went over and stood in front of the window next to the bed.

"Not a typical window view ya find at a bed and breakfast," she mused, arms still crossed. Tripp came up beside her and put a hand on her shoulder. His touch was warm despite how cold the air had become.

"I don't know about you, but it's been a long day."

She turned to him without saying anything, wondering which way he meant that.

"We had quite an adventure. Long drive too." He looked up at the stars then back down at her, his breathing becoming slightly faster. He wanted to, she was sure of it. She wanted him to do it, to just kiss her, but he was shy enough to resist after she pulled away once before. Taking a step back, he cracked a smile then walked around the bed to his side and pulled the covers down to climb in. She climbed up into bed and he flopped the covers down over them and fluffed his pillow before laying back on it, his curls draping the fabric. She couldn't help but stare a moment, until he glanced over at her. She looked away quickly, hiding the fact that she was watching him, but he knew. A corner of his mouth curved up into a half smile. Her fingers smoothed her hair behind her ear and she cleared her throat.

"The bed is comfortable, huh?" He wiggled his foot, which was crossed over the other under the covers.

"It is." Her gaze focused out the window as she remained sitting up, rubbing nervousness from the back of her neck.

"Hey." A gentle hand rested on her shoulder.

"Hmm?" She turned to him, almost startled.

"You okay?" He sat up onto his elbows, the covers lowering to his abs.

"Yeah, yeah. I'm actually not tired enough to sleep yet, I don't think."

"Ok." He sat up fully, waiting for an idea of how to pass the time. She laid on her stomach facing the window, feet crossed and in the air. The anklet she wore on her right ankle slid up her calf a bit. He followed suit, lying on his stomach next to her.

"I don't want to keep you up." She rested on her elbows.

"You're not keeping me up. I'm not that tired yet. Getting there, but not there yet." He shrugged and folded his hands in front of him as he fought the urge to touch her.

"I feel lazy; too lazy for a walk out in the cold, but not tired enough to just close my eyes and crash."

He chuckled. "Me too. Yeah, it's cold out. Screw that."

She let a quiet laugh out of her smile. "We could just talk..." She chewed the inside of her cheek as if that idea was almost a question.

"Sure."

"I used to lay out at the beach at night and listen to the waves. It would be pitch black out there except the moon and stars. It reminded me of going to the planetarium when I was a kid. I felt so small out there, surrounded by the whole world, but it was peaceful and I could clear my head." She gazed at the stars as the big sky darkened, smiling at the memory.

"I can't say I've done that at the beach, just been out there at night like that. You'd go alone?"

"Absolutely. Most times, yeah."

"Sounds like a new bucket list item."

"Yes! It should be. It's funny because seeing a twister was on my bucket list."

"Really?" He laughed, tipping over enough for his shoulder to bump into hers.

"Yes, really."

"That just happened to spin right in your direction. You didn't have to go chasin' that one." They laughed at his pun.

"It didn't exactly go as I thought it would," she said with raised brows. "I appreciate your banter."

"Yeah, I'm sure ducking for cover in a storage closet and losing your car wasn't part of the plan." His laughter seized, making light of her situation yet not wanting to upset her.

"Actually, I hate that my car is gone, but the storage closet is definitely something I'll never forget." Her eyes met his and there was a moment of pause before she said, "You happen to always be in the right place at the right time."

"Maybe there's a reason for that."

"What would that be?" she asked, playing coy.

"Maybe the universe was pushing us together." He leaned in, gravitating closer to her.

"I can't think of any other reason."

"Maybe there's a reason for there only being one room available here tonight too." He looked down then over at her, at her parted lips as she stared at him.

"This road trip has been my best decision in a long time."

"And I'm really glad I chose the route I did." His eyes didn't wander this time. He was assuring her he wanted this.

"Me too." She swallowed extensively as he leaned in, his head tilting slightly. His soft lips pressed against hers, mutual lust locking their lips, and butterflies carried her away in a swarm. Her eyes closed and she ran her fingertips over the scruff of his short-trimmed beard as he tucked her wet hair behind her shoulder and took her cheek in the palm of his hand. She had never felt a kiss so romantic and genuine. He was methodical and precise in the way he kissed. He scooched closer, his lips not parting from hers, and when her arm wrapped around his neck, he rolled with her as she situated herself on her back with him overtop her, brushing her hair from her forehead, his elbows on either side of her holding him up. Was this really happening? Her heart was racing faster, the anticipation that had been building up unable to be contained any longer. The way he made her feel in that moment was like fireworks going off brightly on the clearest of nights. The tension between them was breaking and it felt amazing. Just knowing now that he sincerely felt the same way was fulfilling a need, a void within her that hadn't been whole in a long time.

"You've been driving me crazy, Tripp," she whispered, her voice barely a breath.

"Mmhmm." He kissed her lips, her words having barely escaped her lips. His damp hair fell into her face and she loved it, twirling his curls, but she yearned to be touching him everywhere. His touch roamed down her side, down her hip, then he pulled her leg up over him and she felt she had permission to reciprocate. His shoulders were strong as he held himself above her, adjusting his body to fit with hers, which it did, perfectly. She didn't want to seem too easy, making out and groping each other like teenagers, fearful she may lose his respect if they went further. Perhaps they should take it slower, let the feelings of excitement and anticipation linger a bit longer before taking the full leap. He pulled back, studying her face as her smile grew. Maybe he had read her mind, even though she was as hard to read as she thought he was, but he sat up, sitting next to her.

"Everything okay?" she asked, perching onto her elbows.

"Everything's perfect. You're perfect." The tension was building like the air pressure had before that tornado back in Amarillo. There was some natural force pushing them together and she didn't know what was holding her back.

Her less-than-confident smile and shifted gaze toward the window told him she wasn't used to hearing that, but he wanted nothing more than to show her that he meant it by crossing that border with her. She scooched to the edge of the bed and stood, and with her back to him, she walked the few steps to the window where she pulled her hair to one side, twirling it with her finger.

He came up behind her and wrapped his arms around her, with her arms down to her sides. His hair fell forward as he gently kissed the side of her neck and her hands wanted to wander his body, needed to. She grabbed his quads, the only thing she could reach with her arms pinned down, and felt almost limp, submitting to him, closing her eyes at his closeness and taking in the moment. She had waited her whole life for this feeling with someone and she was becoming obsessed with him. His hands slid up her arms and to her shoulders, turning her to face him, and she cupped his face in her hands, wasting no time smashing her lips to his, passion heating again quickly. Her touch grazed his jawline softly, causing their chemistry to ignite into the hottest of flames. She wasn't just drawn to him, she *needed* him, had to have him. The attraction had been too strong since the moment she first laid eyes on him along the roadside. She pulled away, studying his strikingly handsome face a moment, only to find his gaze that was devouring her. She wanted to savor all of this.

"I respect you too much to rush things with you, Aria."

"And I respect that you feel that way. You're a gentleman, Tripp." She had never moved this fast with anyone before. Her lashes fluttered against his skin as she leaned her forehead against his chest.

"How about we try to behave ourselves tonight? I'll even place a pillow between us."

"Yeah, we probably should, huh?" she blurted quickly, looking up at him.

She could tell this was just as difficult for him as it was for her, to just stop after what they had started. She nodded with a smile, although a bit disappointed. She fell asleep first, nestled up against him, the pillow separating them, his arm around her. As badly as he wanted to kiss her angelic face, he left her to dream.

During the night, even with a pillow between them, every time she'd move or roll over, he'd put his arm over her and pull her close. He was still most of the night, squishing that pillow between them. She barely slept a wink, a bit restless, not wanting to miss out on a moment of him lying next to her. So often she was tempted to reach over and touch him, a fear of waking him stopping her. With dawn breaking, light cast its rays across the room and onto the walls through the window . Expecting him to look a bit rough in the early morning light—his hair a bit tangled and crazy, his scruff leading in different directions—she was pleasantly surprised to see that he still looked perfect. Absolutely perfect. She stared at him, memorizing every feature until he began to wake. She quickly turned her head to the right, slamming her eyes closed and pretending to sleep. She could feel his stare and wanted so badly to see the look on his face as her messy self was waking next to him. With a deep inhale, she rolled to her left side and her eyelids fluttered open. She added a stretch and moan for dramatic effect, causing him to smile as their stares connected. He adjusted the pillow under his curly head, one arm under it. The extra five o'clock shadow added to the scruff he already had and she found it irresistible. Wanting to remain there next to each other all day, it was difficult to force themselves out of bed to carry on with the day.

Mile Marker 10: From Kasha to Albuquerque

"I've read about a cool stop if you wanna check it out. We can get some awesome photos too."

"Sure!"

"Can you look up the directions to Kasha-Katuwe Tent Rocks for me? I've never been to that park but I know we're heading in the right direction."

"Of course. I've never heard of the place so I'm excited to check it out."

"Kasha-Katuwe means 'white cliffs' due to the light color." Tripp pointed at the park photo on Aria's phone.

"That's in Keresan, right?"

"It is. I'm impressed you knew that."

She laughed and turned her phone to face him. "It's on the website."

The park didn't disappoint, either, especially from the bluff trails leading around the top of the five-thousand-acre formation. They viewed cone-shaped tent rocks which formed from volcanic eruptions millions of years ago, composed of soft pumice and tuff cones, and harder stone caprocks. No dogs were allowed, but thanks to Tripp having Atlas service dog certified, Atlas was able to experience the hike. They even visited the Veteran's Memorial at the end of the gravel road overlooking the canyon. The natural landscape was amazing as cone-shaped rock formations stood tall; ninety feet for some and picture perfect. Nature is impressive. Aria had a grip on Tripp's arm on a narrow stretch of trail that was along a cliff edge, but he didn't seem to mind. In fact, he was doing a horrible job at hiding a smirk so, with a wink, he helped to relieve her scared expression. "It's okay! I've got you!"

They stopped at a popular Mexican restaurant in Albuquerque to grab a bite to eat on their patio and plan their next few stops. The waitress came over to their corner booth to take their drink order, returning with them and baskets of chips with salsa and queso. Tripp and Aria browsed the menu while chatting and snacking on the appetizer.

"What are you gonna get?" Tripp asked, skim-reading.

"I'm sticking to my usual. Same thing I get at every Mexican restaurant."

"What's that?"

"Soft chicken tacos."

"Sounds good. You don't like to mix it up and try new stuff?"

"Once in a while, but I usually end up regretting not getting tacos."

He chuckled and closed the menu, setting it on the table. "Fair enough."

"You're welcome to try some of mine if you'd like. That way you don't have to have regrets," Tripp offered after they placed their orders, smiling as he looked up at her before shoving a cheese-coated chip in his mouth. Tongue-in-cheek, she tried thinking of something smartass to say about his joking at her expense, but she was thinking more about wanting to lick the cheese drip from his chin. She chugged her strawberry margarita to distract herself.

"I'm sorry, Aria. You know I was joking, right?"

She set her glass down and swallowed. "Yeah, of course." She added a giggle, realizing her attempt at distracting herself came off as irritated to him. She motioned for him to wipe his chin, and he grabbed a napkin, laughing as he cleaned himself up just as the waiter brought their food out and set the hot plates in front of them.

"Looks delicious. Thank you," Tripp told the waiter. The waiter nodded and walked away as Tripp scooped up a forkful and offered it to Aria.

"Try it." His puppy dog eyes tried convincing her.

She asked, "What's in it?"

"No refried beans or sour cream." He shrugged and she shook her head, passing on his offer.

"You feel like hitting Vegas?" Tripp asked, smoothly changing the subject and glancing down at the plan notes on his phone.

"I'm not a city girl, so..."

"So, it wouldn't break your heart if we didn't detour?"

"Nope. But if it's on your list—"

"Perfect. I was hoping you'd say no."

Aria laughed and gave him a one-shoulder shrug. "So why'd you ask then?"

"I know you don't get to travel often, so being this close, I wanted you to have the opportunity." He shoved another salsa-covered chip in his mouth and she smiled with her chin in her hand and elbow on the table.

"That's kind of you."

He looked up at her after setting his beer down. "What?"

"You're a thoughtful guy. That's all." Her eyes shied away as she lifted her margarita glass to her lips. It was quiet for a moment before he said, "I kinda wish we were traveling through here in the fall."

"Why's that?"

"We could've photographed and blogged the hot air balloon festival," he answered excitedly.

"That would've been cool to see."

"I've always wanted to. Maybe someday."

"Yeah, hopefully. Gives you another excuse to travel back out this way."

Without making eye contact, he asked, "Would you wanna come along?"

"Are you kidding? Yeah, of course! You just won't get me up into one of those things."

He chuckled. "That's fair."

"You aren't claustrophobic, are you?" He dipped a chip in queso.

"Why?" she asked slowly, her eyes narrowing. He chuckled and tossed Atlas a piece of steak from his plate then tried to throw her off-topic by once again offering her a taste of his dish.

She ate the bite and wrinkled her nose a few chews in.

"Really, what's in that?"

"You don't like it?" He took another bite as she cleared her throat and shook her head. He shuffled through his plate with his fork.

"Lettuce, tomatoes, cheese, steak, peppers, rice..."

"Maybe it's the rice," she said before clearing her throat again.

"I guess there are onions and guac too."

"Guacamole?"

"Yeah."

"Oh, shit!" She panicked, eyes wide and dropping the fork with a loud ting.

"What? You don't like guac?" Tripp's brows wrinkled at her loud reaction and he looked around at people staring. Aria coughed into the crook of her elbow.

"I'm not trying to act extreme but—" She coughed again.

"Aria? Are you okay?" He started to feel concerned, flopping his napkin onto the table and patting her back.

"I'm allergic to avocado." She took a drink of her margarita to ease the tingle starting in the back of her throat as he stood quickly and waved the waiter over to the table to pay. Aria insisted on taking her tacos in a go-bag and the waiter hustled, helping them wrap things up at the table.

"Aria, we can worry about food later, we need to get you to the hospital." For the sake of expediency, he slapped a handful of cash, more than enough to cover the bill and tip, on the table and took Aria by the arm to pull her from the booth.

"Do we need to call 9-1-1?" the waiter asked, and Aria shook her head no.

"I'll be okay. I just need my pill. I should have one out in my purse."

"I can drive faster than the ambulance, anyway," Tripp said, gathering the go-bags into one bag so they were easier to carry. Aria grabbed the dog's leash and they rushed to the car. "Next time, I'll get the sizzling fajitas."

She laughed then coughed as she frantically rummaged through her purse. Tripp loaded Atlas and the food into the Jeep before himself and searched for the nearest hospital on his phone.

"There's a drug store not far. It's too late for the Minute-Clinic, but they should have something for your reaction. You have an EpiPen?"

"No, I don't. I thought I had a pill in here. Dammit." She coughed again and reached for a bottle of water on the floor of the Jeep. "I doubt I have one in my luggage."

"Sounds like you need a hospital. There's one not much farther." Tripp hit the pedal hard, revving the motor as they flew down Route 66. "There's one in three miles. You going to be okay until then?"

"I hope so. I found one pill." Her breathing was becoming more labored as the medicine wasn't taking effect fast enough, and he kept glancing over at her the whole three miles, making sure she wasn't unconscious or turning blue. He even took hold of her hand on the console, thinking it might help keep her calm. Atlas whined from the back seat, sensing something was wrong. Tripp's heart was racing just as much as hers, if not harder. Whipping the Jeep into the hospital parking lot, tires squealed on the pavement. He slammed it into park and hauled ass to her side of the Jeep, taking only a few minutes to get her inside the emergency room, the bright red-lit sign glowing in the night. She was checked in and called back to a room right away. Her allergic reaction took precedence over those waiting in the lobby. Tripp quickly explained to the nurse what was going on as breathing became more difficult for Aria. The nurse left the room for a brief moment, returning with an epinephrine shot. Aria's arm took the needle harshly but then she relaxed, able to breathe better within minutes. They thanked the staff as she was released as soon as the discharge paperwork was completed. Heading back out to the Jeep, Tripp hung his head.

"It's my fault."

"What? No, it's not."

"I fed you something you're allergic to. So yeah, it is my fault."

"Tripp, you didn't know. I didn't come right out and say I have a food allergy."

"I should've told you what all was in it before feeding it to you. I don't even think I read the description on the menu."

"Don't be silly. You saved me with the pedal to the metal." She laughed and it turned into a cough but not as harsh or frequent as moments prior.

"This medicine always knocks me out, by the way, so you don't have to freak out if I fall asleep."

"Good to know. I'm still going to be keeping a close eye on you all night."

Aria smiled at how sweet he was, wondering if he's just this way or if he feels protective over her specifically. Either way, he had been so good to her.

She had fallen asleep by the time they reached a hotel just a half mile from a hospital. After checking in, he let Atlas into the room and took their bags in before going back out for Aria. He tried waking her but she was out cold so he carried her in and laid her on a bed, then covered her up before showering. She seemed to be breathing normally so, worrying less, he got comfortable on the other bed with Atlas at his feet. Every time Tripp would doze off, he'd startle himself awake again, worried, and would check on her.

Aria woke the next morning to Tripp and Atlas coming in from outside. Her eyes squinted open and she stretched an arm.

"Sorry. I tried not to make noise. He couldn't wait," he apologized.

"It's okay. What time is it?"

"Nine." He unhooked Atlas's leash from the collar.

"Oh! I'm sorry I slept in so late."

"Don't be. You needed the rest."

She sat up, looking around.

"How did I—"

"I carried you in. You weren't waking up. Hope that's okay."

"Yeah, yeah of course. Sorry 'bout that."

"No need to be sorry, Aria. *I'm* sorry."

She stood from the bed, fully clothed still.

"Really, you don't need to be sorry. Allergies just happen and that's not on you. Besides, I'm fine thanks to you."

"I was really worried about you." He slung his duffle bag strap over his shoulder, ready to load it into the Jeep.

"Aww, you're sweet. She sniffed her shirt on her way over to her bag sitting in the office chair.

He chuckled. "I'm in no hurry. Take a shower if you need to. I'm going to take my bag out and fill the cooler with fresh ice, then I'll be back. Oh, I'll grab us bagels from the lobby too."

"Okay, I'll hustle. Gosh, why didn't you tell me I smell like the restaurant?" She took wrinkled clothes out of her bag and headed for the shower.

He laughed, checking the map on his phone on his way out.

Mile Marker 11: The Wave

"So, this is one spot I've always wanted to visit." Tripp led the way on foot through the park entrance.

"I've seen pictures of this place." Aria looked around at the terracotta walls surrounding them.

"It's called The Wave; a perfect scenic hiking spot. It's a popular rock-climbing spot too."

"Believe it or not, I have gone rock climbing before."

Tripp stopped in his tracks, gravel shifting beneath him as he turned to her with wide eyes.

"You what?"

She laughed and took his hand, continuing to walk.

"It was in a gym and I barely made it twenty feet up before returning to the shame awaiting below."

His head tipped back in laughter.

"Hey, it counts!" She slapped his arm playfully.

"You're right, it does. This is a different ballgame though. Since it's summer and so damn hot, we shouldn't be out here all day."

"We have plenty of water, snacks in our bags, and misting fans. I was hoping to stay until dark to see the Milky Way. It's supposed to be epic out here."

"I mean...if you wanna try, I'm down for that." Tripp shrugged.

"I wanna try." She batted her eyes and that's all it took for him to comply with her starry wishes. "Oh! I have something for you." She fished around in the side of the camera bag and pulled out a folding tactical knife. Handing it to him, she said, "I didn't really leave my sunglasses in the TeePee shop."

He took it from her and flipped it open. The black stonewashed finished handle had a road map design and the stainless-steel blade had a compass rose laser engraved on both sides.

"Aria...this is a beautiful knife." He looked at her, a pleasant surprise on his face. "You saw this in there and went back in to buy it?"

"I did. I had to."

"It's perfect. Thank you." He wrapped his arms around her, adding a kiss to her forehead, but Atlas was itching to keep moving.

The day was long and the sun was hot. The layered walls provided only a little shade every so often. Sweat was beading on his brow and she was overheating with her hair down so she used her hair clip to keep it up, allowing air to reach her neck. She took an ice cube from their small cooler, rubbing it all over her neck, then ran it across her collarbones to instantly feel cooler. She knew this trick increased blood flow to the brain and would slow her racing heart rate. Watching her with a loose jaw, Tripp's blood began flowing elsewhere. He needed a distraction so brought up a conversation topic that he thought fitting as he fiddled with an old compass from his bag, teaching her how it worked.

"My grandpa passed away last year. He gave me this when he became ill. I rushed back from my last road trip to be by his side when he passed."

"I'm so sorry, Tripp. The compass is beautiful. It's nice you have this memento of his." She took it, looking it over before handing it back to him.

"Yeah. Ya know, he was never wrong about anything. Ever.

His advice was always brilliant, his predictions were always spot on. It was like he could—"

"See the future?"

"Almost, in a way. When I was younger, I used to think people who thought they had psychic abilities were a bit..." He shrugged and looked down at the antique compass.

"Crazy?"

"I guess so. But he made me second guess all of it. He was such a jokester, a real smartass. He'd tell me stories about when he was in World War Two and he was such a badass; surviving sinking ships, planes going down, malaria four times and being treated by the aborigines in New Guinea. Anyway, he used to say stuff that didn't really make sense yet did at the same time." He adjusted more comfortably on the rock they were sitting on. "Okay, for example, he used to say, 'No matter where ya go, there ya are.'"

"What?" She couldn't help but chuckle.

"Exactly. He'd say it in a serious tone then laugh and wink when I'd look confused. It was hard to tell when he was joking sometimes. He was a bit of a dry humor guy."

"Must run in the family," she joked, bumping into his arm. He laughed.

"The point is, it doesn't matter where I go in the world because I'll always be with myself so I have to be the kind of person I'd want to be around. I have to count on myself. I need to *be* a person others would want to be around. I can't run away from my problems and fears, I have to sit with them and face them no matter where I am. Once I started traveling, that all started making sense. I'll never be truly lost if I always know where to find myself and I would never have to look too hard if I just follow my heart and be who I truly am."

"It's like he wanted you to understand that clue on your own."

"He told me when he got sick that I would find my soulmate during my travels. I'd see her, I'd want to get to know her, and I'd fall in love with her. She would be the reason for my fate as a traveler. I put that compass wheel cover on the back of my Jeep as a tribute to him originally; for him to in a way guide me, maybe even to keep me safe, I don't know. Maybe I was led to you. Maybe we crossed paths and kept crossing paths because we were supposed to."

"The compass necklace?" She held the pendant in her fingertips and looked up at him. "I don't know what to make of all of this, Tripp. He may have been onto something."

"I know it sounds crazy, but I have felt exactly the way he said I would. Only with you."

"What if you're wasting time with me and it's not me that you're supposed to be with?"

"Well, I don't believe that. I acted on how I feel in my heart; how I have this whole time. I've been led to you and I think you've been led right into my path of fate."

"Maybe that's where I *was* directed."

"I truly believe that. I think I was being directed to you and redirected to you, again and again. I think I'm on this road trip and on this route for a reason. That tire had to blow and that tornado needed to pass through and you needed my help...all of it. Things *do* happen for a reason. Maybe Grandpa passed away when he did in order to send you to me."

"I think we owe him a big thank you when we're looking up to the heavens tonight, thanking our lucky stars."

"I think we do."

Atlas had a blast exploring but not wandering too far from them. They took advice from previous travelers on how to take stunning photos and sat against a darkening wall waiting for the sky to become dark enough to be able to see the Milky Way. Not only did they see it, they took amazing photos of it; the blues, purples, and pinks that lit the sky were breathtaking, especially through the camera lens, and the stars were glittery specks of brilliant white. They laid back on the floor of the walled trail, quietly gazing up at the sky. His focus changed to her, watching her stargaze in all her beauty.

"What are you thinking about?" he asked, adjusting his hands behind his head for comfortability.

Before she shifted her gaze to him, she answered, "I'm thinking I can put together a time-lapse video from our photos here."

His smile grew large as he looked back up at the sky. Her body shifted so she was on her side, his bag bunched up under her head, facing him.

"What were you thinking about?" Her smirk showed anticipation for knowing his answer and it took a moment of pause before he looked at her.

"I was thinking this would be a perfect moment for kissing you."

"Then why aren't you?" Her lips parted slightly, inviting him to move in closer. He accepted her invitation, slowly, memorizing her face as he got closer before his lips melted to hers for a spark-flying kiss. His hand roamed her body, slowly and gently; the arch of her hip working him up, until he was barely able to keep control. He was a romantic, which was what she longed for in a relationship. He was exactly what she needed, she just hadn't known it until she met him. She suddenly recalled advice a friend once gave her: once you feel the nervous butterflies and the racing heartbeat with someone, you've found someone special. She felt exactly all of that as he cupped her face in his hands, up on an elbow, and felt the earth beneath them.

Mile Marker 12: Coral Pink Sand Dunes

"Where to today?" Aria asked, tossing her bag into the Jeep.

"Well, how about Coral Pink Sand Dunes? I hadn't planned it originally but why the hell not?" Tripp refreshed the cooler with ice outside of Red Canyon Cabins.

"Sounds good to me."

"I have another adventure in mind." He grinned as he shut the back door of the Jeep.

"You aren't going to tell me what it is either, are you?" she asked, climbing into the passenger side as he got in the driver's.

"Nope." That grin spread wider as he adjusted his ball cap and started the Jeep, driving away from those tiny cabins and that red canyon postcard scenery.

"You were right about sunup being beautiful out here."

"I'm surprised you were willing to get up so early after we were out late last night." Tripp took his coffee thermos from the cup holder.

"Yeah, well...I couldn't sleep well anyway. You know we could've saved money by sharing a two-bed cabin." Aria put her hair back into a hair tie.

Tripp froze a moment, thermos still at his lips, before saying, "I could've asked you if you're okay with that, but I didn't wanna make it sound like...ya know." He took a sip.

"Didn't wanna seem too pushy?" She snickered. He almost choked on his coffee.

"What's so funny?"

He set his thermos back in the cupholder and wiped his bottom lip with the back of his hand.

"Yeah. Pushy."

"Saving money isn't being pushy, Tripp."

"I know, but I didn't want you to think I was looking for more than that."

"I wasn't implying that you wanted intimacy."

He whipped his head to look at her in surprise.

"Oh my God, you should see the look on your face right now." She couldn't hold back the laughter that bubbled out of her.

"What look? I don't have a look." He shied away, looking forward at the road ahead.

"You did so. I just can't tell if that was a look of horror or surprise, or even—"

"Surprise, I guess."

"I like that you're shy. It's attractive." She watched his confused reaction; his brows turned in and looked out the driver window before asking, "Why do you say I'm shy?"

"Oh, Tripp."

"And I'm surprised you find it attractive. I guess I'm just a private person. I don't know." He seemed flustered and she found it adorable.

"An introvert?" She tilted her head, assessing him.

He shrugged. "Yeah, I guess. I lack the *need* for conversation most of the time."

"Is that why you travel alone?"

"I'm not alone. I have Atlas. And you too, for this trip."

She smiled.

"There was a colleague that would travel on partial trips with me sometimes. He was the photographer for the magazine. But in general, I'm not really the most social person. This really is the perfect job for me. I uh...I have bad anxiety, especially in crowds or under the pressure of a busy workplace. Teaching classes was crowd enough. That's why Atlas is a service dog. I just don't force him to wear the harness when I have his paperwork."

"This job suits you well then. And that's okay. I'm not super social either, to be honest. I'm glad you have Atlas looking out for you."

He looked at her, surprise etched into his features once again.

"Could've fooled me...about you not being social."

She laughed. "Really, I'm not. I have work, where I get along with everyone, and my close circle of friends. I don't go places to meet new people."

"You seemed comfortable with me right away though," he pointed out.

"That's because I was...after my nervous shakes dissipated. Okay, actually, I still get that feeling around you sometimes but it's a good thing. I almost fumble on words, we both have a hard time keeping eye contact with each other for long. I don't know why I look away because I don't want to. I could stare at you all day and all night. Your shy smile makes me just wanna..."

"Wanna what?"

"Kiss you." She smirked, shying her eyes away again. "You weren't exactly sure about me though, were you?" She stared him down, trying to read him like a book, but he had mystery to his magnetic, radiating charm.

"Actually, I liked you right away, but I don't know about comfortable."

"Hmmm?"

"I mean, I trusted you, sure, but I've been nervous around you."

"And shy. A total gentleman though."

He laughed. "Okay, yeah. Shy too."

"Why?" She put her foot up on the dash, drawing his attention.

He cleared his throat and adjusted the seatbelt across his chest, a tell-tale sign of nervousness.

"Because I obviously find you attractive too."

"Is that so?" She sat up, throwing in a teasing lip bite that made him grin uncontrollably.

"Yeah." He chuckled, shaking his head.

"I feel relieved." She sat back, slouching, relaxed.

"What? Why?" His eyes darted between the road and her.

"Because I thought the same of you the very first second I saw you as you approached my car on the side of the road. I've felt nervous around you too, not knowing if you felt the same way."

"Seriously?"

"Oh yeah," she said in a sultry tone that made him clear his throat again. "I'm not sure why you're surprised, Tripp. You've seen yourself in the mirror." Her focus shied to the passenger window view of the red sand surrounding them, and his attention was on her, those eyes of hers watching his reflection.

"Hmm, well, I guess I'll just have to show you shy later."

"And there's my nervous shakes again." Heat flooded her pink cheeks. For the rest of the drive, she was fantasizing about this stranger sitting next to her. She had a hard time looking away from him when his attention was on the road, scoping him out with peripheral vision in play.

After stopping for breakfast on the go, they pulled into an ATV rental place at the Coral Pink Sand Dunes stop. Atlas followed them in, and was even fitted for goggles as Tripp and Aria rented theirs with the four-person dune buggy.

"I figure we'd give these new body cams a try," Tripp said as he buckled Atlas in the back seat harness.

"That's adorable and hilarious." Aria laughed as she snapped her body cam in place.

"Yeah? Well, you're really going to laugh at this then." Tripp snapped a body cam to the front of Atlas's collar and it dangled below his slobbery chin as he panted, anxious for the ride.

"I love it. We'll probably need to take Dramamine before watching it later." Aria laughed.

"Probably so," Tripp agreed, laughing as he offered for her to drive, but she shook her head no. Tripp's driving style was definitely different than when he drove the Jeep. He drove that ATV like a bat out of Hell. The terrain was rough, causing Aria to grab the door for stability. Flying across the red clay, jumping hills and drifting, the sand flew. The loud motor didn't cover the sound of her screaming and laughing, having a blast. The dune buggy finally twirled to a stop and Tripp unbuckled right out in the middle of nowhere. They wiped dirt off of their goggles with a dirt-covered rag that had been tied to a rail on the buggy and all three gulped water, rinsing down dirt with it.

"Your turn." Tripp walked over to the passenger side.

"What?"

"Go ahead. Drive. Ya can't roll it, there's a cage. Well, technically you can, but it'll be fine. We're fine."

"Oh, I—"

"Scooch over. Let's see whatcha got."

"Okay, why not?" She slid over behind the wheel and buckled up before she hit the gas.

"There's nothing out here but dirt! Don't be afraid to gas it!" Tripp yelled over the loudness of the motor. Her eyes squinted shut a moment, white knuckles gripping the wheel as she floored it.

"Yeah! That's what I'm talking about!" Tripp's fist banged the dash, encouraging her to cut loose. Atlas barked with excitement. That dog was just as adventurous as Tripp. Once they drove the ATV back to the building, he hoisted her up, wrapping her around him as they kissed, tasting salt on each other's lips, sharing dirt, and wearing each other's sweat, which bothered neither one of them at all. Dirt poofed from their hair as he let her down. His arms were smeared with dirt, then his forehead, from wiping the sweat from his brow. They carried their dirt-blasted goggles inside after knocking their shoes off on the porch as Atlas sucked down water from a bowl out by the Jeep.

"Looks like you folks had a good time." The gentleman at the desk laughed.

"We did, thanks," Tripp said, handing the key over. Aria nodded in agreement, a proud smile on her dirty face.

"We do have private showers if you two wanted to clean up before heading out," the gentleman offered.

Tripp turned to Aria with brows raised and tossed his curls, sending a cloud of dirt into the air around his head. She coughed and laughed, entertained by his not-so-subtle cue.

"Showers it is. I think I'll hose down Atlas first." Tripp gestured for her to exit the building ahead of him to grab clean clothes from the Jeep. She showered while he hosed the dog down, then she waited out next to the Jeep so the dog could air dry until Tripp came out...in a snug white t-shirt and cargo shorts, his hair dripping wet. She couldn't help but stare at him. Was he walking in slow motion? It sure seemed like it. He opened the back for Atlas to hop in, then got in and started the Jeep, rolling the window down to ask Aria, "You ready?" as she tried to pick her jaw up off the ground.

"Yeah, I'm good." She hustled into the Jeep and had to look away from him a moment to take a deep breath.

"You okay?" he asked, driving off.

"Mmhmm." He had no idea what he was doing to her.

"You sure?"

Attempting to look at those brown eyes again, all she could do was nod and smile.

They entered the hotel, Aria in a rush as she helped him carry their bags inside. She took hold of the front of his shirt, pulling his lips to hers as she pushed him backward a few steps until his back hit the wall. His hand wrapped up in her hair, the other sliding down to her ass cheek. He turned her around so her back was against the wall and removed his shirt, his touch roaming south before he took her by the hand, leading her over next to the bed. He was going to be quenching her thirst for him finally. The anticipation had been too much for him to bear, and now that the passion was burning, there would be no stopping them.

"Where have you been all my life?" He pushed her hair back behind her shoulder so lightly, as if it would break like thin glass, but when she snaked her fingers through his curls, he stepped backward a few steps, bringing her with him until the back of his leg touched the bed and he sat. Holding on to her waist and looking up at her, he didn't say a word, but he didn't need to. Those brown eyes of his were needy, but he was patient as she stood, admiring how perfect he was. Her fluttering lashes had his full attention. Taking hold of his shoulders, she straddled him slowly, one leg at a time. He grabbed her legs and slid her closer, as close as she could possibly be. She felt him grow harder, which turned her on even more, him pulsating against her, even through his shorts. Desire flared in her emerald green eyes as her head angled to melt her lips with his. He quickly took the kiss deeper, breaths becoming heavy as they gave in to the temptation they both had been fighting. A hot breath trailed down her neck and had her arching backward, her lower back being held as the trail led to her chest, then mercilessly claimed her lips again as he pulled her in closer to him. He sure knew how to make a girl turn to complete mush. Grinding against him, fully clothed, she wanted him inside her so badly, but the anticipation and teasing felt so good too. Tripp flipped her, laying her on the bed, stripping her bottoms off after she removed her shirt, remaining positioned between her legs, one foot on the floor. With his hair falling to either side of his face, she couldn't resist the urge to feel his curls against her hand. He stood, stripped his shorts off, letting them fall to the floor, presenting himself to her. Using his masculine shoulders to hold his weight above her, he watched her eyes scan his body. He was impressive, every inch of him. Her fingertips slid down his collarbone, which hovered directly above her, then down his chest as her gaze held his. His lips curled into a smile when she bit her lip with anticipation. Her chest rose then fell as he lowered to kiss her lips, gently, softly, passionately. He weaved his fingers with hers, raising and pinning her arms above her head against the plush pillow, sinking into the fluff, her eyes closed as he kissed his way to her chest, low enough that he was forced to release her hands. His back felt strong, shoulder blades protruding as he kept himself raised just above her body; tauntingly so. She craved for him to be against her so badly, inside her even more. She gave his hair a tug, signalling him to bring his gaze to hers. He crawled back up to eye level. Tongues tangoed and his brows raised with surprise as she felt her way down to his toned glutes. She pulled him close, her nails digging in just enough. He took that as a cue that she was ready for him and entered her slowly, eliciting a moan from between his lips. Her breath hitched at the pressure of him entering her, demanding he thrust harder by burrowing her nails a little deeper into his flesh. She let her kisses move to his jaw then down the side of his neck. His smooth rolling motions, the way the front of his hips pressed against hers, drove her crazy. He touched the side of her face so gently, his eyes looking into hers a moment, into her soul, before his gaze moved to her lips. Tracing his fingers along her body, as if he were following lines on a map, was so incredibly sexy. As his lips brushed across hers and teased kisses down her neck, her back arched, pressing her breasts against his toned chest, merging their bodies and rhythm into one. She wrapped her hand up in his hair, not wanting him to stop. Electrifying tingles shot up her spine as he made her feel like no one else ever had. She was addicted to him, she craved him, he was easily making her obsessed with the way he showed affection. She wanted the constant skin-to-skin contact to never break, nor the bond they had created. Their limbs tangled and a corner of the sheet came untucked from the mattress with the friction of their bodies. Pushing him in deeper as her legs squeezed, wrapping around him, he obliged to every whim she signaled, or didn't signal, and took his time making sure she was satisfied. His scruff against her skin didn't feel as rough as she imagined. She tried to memorize everything about him: every muscle curve, his chest tattoo, every facial feature. He was perfect. Mapping him out, she didn't want to forget a thing. Everything about this, everything about him, just felt right, like it wasn't just inevitable, but meant to be; a fateful connection.

Mile Marker 13: Grand Canyon

D ust settled as the tires of the Jeep rolled to a stop.

"I figured we could do the touristy thing before we go find our own secluded spot. Is that okay?" Tripp asked as he put the Jeep into park and raked his hair back into a tie.

"That sounds perfect."

Tripp clipped the leash onto Atlas's collar and they all climbed out of the Jeep together.

"Think we can get over the clear bridge and drive back around the secluded spot before sunset?" he asked, taking her hand as they began walking.

"We have almost two hours before sunset so prob—" She stopped in her tracks, the sudden motion jerking her hand out of his.

"What's wrong? You okay?" He adjusted his ball cap, using it to block the sun as he scanned for danger.

"Did you say clear bridge? As in *glass*?" She spoke in a higher octave, making him smile and fight the urge to laugh.

"Yeah. The view is amazing from there."

She looked around nervously, jittery, her heart starting to race and her feet seemingly frozen to the ground in spite of the desert heat. She gulped a swallow before he asked, "Aria, are you—"

"Afraid of heights? Yes. Deathly terrified." She inhaled then exhaled a deep breath.

"I didn't know. I'm sorry." His expression turned more concerned.

"It's okay. I don't wanna slow you down. Sometimes I just need a little push. Not literally!"

"We don't need to rush. Or we can rush if you'd rather. We can find another view; I just know that this is a really cool spot. I don't want you to regret not checking it out."

"This may be the only chance I get to see it though." She chewed the inside of her cheek, trying to convince herself to be brave, then looked at him.

"I don't want to freak out on you or faint or something."

"I will hold your hand the whole time."

"How will you take photos then though? You have the leash."

"Either you can take the leash or take the pics."

"I'm no photographer so..."

"Neither am I, technically. Maybe you taking the photos will give you something else to concentrate on and you'll be facing a fear at the same time." He shrugged both shoulders dramatically.

"I'd rather the photos turn out well for you."

"They will. Come on, what do ya say? Wanna conquer that fear? Together?"

She huffed a deep exhale and looked at those begging brown eyes...Atlas's and Tripp's.

"You know bad luck follows me, Tripp. What if—"

He shook his head no, interrupting her anxiety spiral.

"Everything always turns out okay."

"Only because of you. Without you, I'd be a victim of some freak accident. It's as though there's an invisible force field around you, protecting you from any harm. There must be, right?"

"I'm just careful, so I'll help you be careful too. I'll be right beside you. I'd really like for you to experience this but I won't force you, of course." He held a hand out.

"Promise you won't let go of me?"

"I promise."

She paused a few more seconds then took his hand. Her nervous expression turned brave and she even managed to crack a smile, but only because he did. He was proud of her.

She had a nauseous feeling in her stomach, that somersault feeling, and had a death grip on Tripp's hand, her knuckles white and his almost purple from the tightness of her grip as they stepped onto the overlook.

"Oh my God!" She looked down, starting to visibly tremble.

"Hey, it's okay. I've got you. Maybe looking out would be better than looking down." He used the leashed hand to point out over the canyon.

"I don't know if I can do this." She turned to him.

"Look at me, beautiful. You've survived everything life has thrown at you this last week."

"I'm sure life isn't done throwing either."

He chuckled. "I'll be right here with you. You've got this. Of course it's smart to be aware of dangers, it's instinct, actually, but to live your life in fear is...this will be fun."

"Easy for you to say. You're not afraid of anything."

"Sure I am."

"Really?"

"Yeah, absolutely. Everyone is afraid of something. Life is delicate for each and every one of us."

"Could've fooled me."

"Why do you say that?"

"I bet you're an adrenaline junkie. You don't just look fear in the eyes, you go after everything that would terrify most people like it's a challenge, don't you?"

"I guess so. I like challenges. You haven't seen anything yet." He chuckled and squeezed her arm. They walked arm-in-arm behind several small groups of tourists. She was almost leading him, rushing to get it over with as they passed a few groups. She took a deep breath, relaxing as they reached the other end of the bridge. Her fear of heights was an evaporating thought for the time being.

"See? All is good. You survived." He couldn't contain a smartass grin.

"I'm convinced it's because you're here."

"I doubt you would've come here if I hadn't pressured you, not over the bridge anyway."

"You're right, I wouldn't have. I did want to see the canyon though. I'm glad you were here with me. It made the experience special...and safer."

"Aww you're sweet." He kissed her forehead. "I know I wouldn't be happy with unfulfilled dreams or wanna die with an empty bucket, no list to check off. No single droplet of water runs through the same river twice...or whatever that saying is. Take the chance while you have it I guess is what I'm trying to say."

"You're right. I need to suck it up and trust you. Tripp. You have rushed in to save me every time I've needed saving. It's like you don't think of the danger, you just...help."

"I do think of the danger though. I guess I just assess the situation and think of a solution fast. I don't know. It seems easy with you."

"Why? Why with me?" she asked, suddenly dwelling on the fact that he called her beautiful.

"I think of your safety first. That just comes naturally."

"Tell me then, if not tornadoes or heights, what are you afraid of?"

He sat and put his head down, his elbows on his knees, picking apart a blade of desert grass.

"I'm afraid that when I drop you off at your house...I'm afraid I'll never see you again. I can't imagine being oceans apart or having deserts separating us as I head back out on the road, leaving you behind...I want to be *with* you. I want to move mountains with you."

She crouched down, looking him in the eyes, and softly touched his arm.

"Oh, Tripp. I was afraid of that too; that I'd never see you again. I want to be with you too." She could tell it took courage for him to share his fear.

He dropped the blade of grass and tucked her hair behind her shoulder, gazes locked.

"Now that I know we have that same fear, I'm not so afraid anymore."

"Me either." She grabbed his face and kissed him, sweet but fierce.

"I guess I am afraid of falling in love and getting hurt too."

"I won't hurt you, Tripp, so go right on ahead."

His brows raised with his cheeks as he smiled.

"Now let's go get some great shots of this canyon," she said, giving his chest a pat.

After taking photos of the breathtaking scenery, they headed back to the Jeep, watching a chopper flying low over them.

"Okay, so I have a surprise for you." Tripp scooped her arm with his in hopes she wouldn't freak out.

"I'm not sure I'm going to like your surprise based on the fact you can't look me in the eyes when you spring it on me," Aria said with a giggle.

All Tripp could do was turn his head and laugh as the chopper landed nearby, stirring dust up in a whirlwind.

"We've already been over this scared of heights thing, Tripp!" Aria had a tight hold of Tripp's arm as he led her to the chopper, Atlas following on the leash.

"Yeah, I know. I already had this planned though before I knew that and I think you're better prepared for this than you think. Plus you did say sometimes you just need a little push to do the scary stuff," he hollered back over the loud engine and spinning propellers overhead that they ducked under.

"Really? Um, because I don't feel that way at all. I can't just get over that fear after one scary experience."

"No?"

She looked back at him as she climbed into the chopper and

he smiled. His dry humor was adorable, no matter how nervous she was. He helped Atlas up into the chopper before he climbed in. The pilot handed them headsets as they sat on the narrow benches and Aria wasted no time buckling up before putting hers on. Tripp and the pilot exchanged a few words she couldn't hear over the noise and she had to yell at the top of her lungs to get their attention, "What?"

"Turn your headset on!" Tripp hollered, but Aria's forehead wrinkled as she strained to hear him. He motioned for her to flip the switch on the side of her headset, but then reached over to do it himself.

"Oh!" she shouted, causing Tripp to laugh at the sharp sound ringing in his ears.

"Everyone buckled up and ready to roll?" the pilot asked.

Aria took a deep breath and nodded. Tripp patted the pilot's seat and said, "Let's do it!"

She had her arm locked with his tightly and he loved that she felt safer with him. Atlas sat buckled in across from them, panting but loving the adventure.

"I want to take photos but I don't want to get close to the open door or let go of you." Aria faced him, still grasping his bicep.

"I can take pictures." He leaned forward and reached for the camera bag that was next to Atlas, but she wasn't letting go. He looked back at her with a smile and said, "You might have to loosen your grip for just a quick second."

"Oh! Right." She loosened her hold on his arm but grabbed the back of his shirt until he got the camera from the bag and sat back against the seat. Their arms locked again and he couldn't help but let out a chuckle as he put the camera strap around his neck.

"Don't get too close to the door," she told him.

"I'll be careful," he assured her.

From the chopper, they could see the canyon; layers of color variation in rock formations and the Colorado River snaking through. The impressive result of arid-land erosion was a scenic wonder. Postcards didn't do it justice.

"This really is amazing!" Aria was getting a little braver, her grip on Tripp's arm loosening as she leaned opposite him to look out her door.

"Yeah, it is." Tripp noticed her inching closer to the door and concealed a smile behind the camera as he photographed her silhouette against the scenery, sun lowering in the sky.

The sky erupted in coral colors, shades of fire ripping across the sky as pink and purple clouds hung in the distance. They had driven around in the Jeep after the chopper ride and found the perfect secluded spot.

"Mmm." She pulled away from a kiss and pointed to the sky. "Look at that photo op!"

He chuckled and handed her the camera. With a smile, she took it and adjusted a setting then snapped a perfect photo of the sun setting over the Grand Canyon. Turning the opposite direction, she snapped a photo of their shadows behind them.

"I wanna take a few of you." He held out his hand for the camera and snapped a pooch-perfect shot of Atlas before taking a few of Aria. She'd change poses, making him laugh one minute, then he'd just stare and adore her the next, taking in the way the sunset colors lit up her face. She took a few pics of him but he was being camera shy. She set the camera up with continuous snaps as they had candid fun together, dancing to no music, standing hand-in-hand in the sunset's glory at the edge of the cliff, and him wrapping his arms around her. Their kiss was captured as the orange sun sank below the horizon.

"I wish sunset lasted longer," he said.

"Oh? Why's that?"

"Because you look so beautiful beneath its colors."

"Aww." She pulled him down for a kiss.

"They say places like this bring out the romantic gestures in people." He held her hands as they stood facing each other.

"I've heard that." She was curious as to what he was getting at.

"Yeah? But I think it's more than that."

"What do you mean?"

"I think it makes people realize we aren't here on Earth long so we should jump at opportunities that may only come along once. We should take in all the precious moments like they'll never come around again because they won't. We should tell each other how we really feel because tomorrow isn't promised to any of us and we're constantly reminded of how time flies and how short life can be." He looked down at their hands then back up at her, a twinkle in his eyes. She felt instantly shaky and couldn't hold back an excited smile.

"Aria, I know we haven't known each other long, we just met actually, but I don't wanna wait to tell you how I feel. I think life with you would be the best road trip with so many adventures."

This man had come into her life unexpectedly and blew her away with a new love like she had never felt before, forming an unbreakable bond.

"I can't imagine living life any other way, or with anyone else." She squeezed his hands.

"Good. Because I fell for you as easily and as naturally as simply breathing." He took a deep breath, looking her straight in the sparkling eyes, and said, "Aria, I love you."

Her smile lit the sunset up. "I love you too, Tripp!"

"Yeah?" he asked excitedly.

She nodded. "Yes! I love you!" she shouted, echoing her confession throughout the canyon. He took a small step back, so as to not yell in her ear when he yelled, "I love you, Aria!" He whipped his ball cap around backwards as she stepped to him.

"I stepped into a cactus." His smile dissipated for a moment and he pulled a thorn from his pant leg before taking her giggling face in his hands and kissing her as the sun hid below the farthest canyon wall. Her arms squeezed tightly around his neck, not wanting to let him go, and time stood still as they took in the moment. Atlas barked...then barked again.

"I think he approves. He's picky too," Tripp joked, making Aria laugh.

"Yay! I was so worried." She wiped pretend nervous sweat off her forehead.

"Together, we're going places," he said. Her hands slid down his arms as he took her by the waist and held her close, then slid back up to his shoulders.

"We were meant to find each other, you know that?" She looked into his eyes and wanted to melt when he looked back at her, pure adoration shining from the very depths of his soul.

"I believe that too. There are no coincidences."

"I agree. I do know we only live once, so I want to live it happily...and you, Tripp, you make me happy."

"Good, because I've never been as happy as I've been with you." The way he tangled his hand up in her hair when he kissed her set her heart on fire. Stars were becoming visible and the air had suddenly cooled even though her temperature always rose when she was so close to him.

Mile Marker 14: Arizona Caverns

"Did I just read a billboard that said caverns?" Aria looked in the side mirror then turned around, looking out the back window as Tripp steered the Jeep down an unpaved road. Dust clouded her view so she turned back around in her seat, catching Tripp in a snicker.

"Tripp?" she asked, hand on the dash steadying her.

"Good thing I have two headlamps."

"Um...what? Hea-headlamps?" Aria's words stumbled out nervously.

"It's okay. This will be fun." Tripp sounded enthused as he flung the Jeep into park and patted her knee before exiting excitedly. She paused a brief moment, wide-eyed, before jumping out of the Jeep and hustling to the back where Tripp retrieved his hiking bag. Atlas waited, panting and wagging his nub as Tripp dug headlamps out of a bag in the back.

"You're both adrenaline junkies. I knew it!" Aria accused, pointing a finger at the two of them.

Tripp laughed and said, "You will be too by the time the road trip is over."

She stared at him with panic in her eyes.

"It's important to face your fears anyway. Think of it like ripping off a bandage really fast." He slung his bag onto his back then crouched down to hook Atlas's leash. It took her a moment to follow because her feet felt glued to the ground. Atlas looked back and stopped, refusing to continue onward without her. He barked and she swallowed hard before walking. Tripp stopped and let her catch up.

"I'll stay by your side the whole time."

"I appreciate that but that won't prevent the cavern from caving in."

Tripp smiled and bumped her shoulder with his arm, looking at her. "I thought you were looking forward to adventure on your vacation? I won't push, though, if you don't want to try this."

She looked over at him, worry swimming in her eyes.

"I'll do it...I just have to panic first."

"That's the last thing you should do. Save the adrenaline for the actual adventure." He put an arm around her for comfort as they entered the entrance to the cavern. A guide met them along the roped trail at the opening and handed them each a helmet before explaining the rules and history of the caverns. Tripp put his extra headlamp around Atlas's collar since their helmets had one. Aria clipped hers to the belt loop on her jeans. Between not being able to see the entrance anymore and the cavern ceiling being low in some areas, Aria felt the need to keep a death grip on Tripp's arm unless she was stopped to take photos.

"This is really cool," she said, observing the spikes hanging from above.

"See...I told you it would be cool."

"It's still confining though."

"You're not freaking out so you're doing fine." Tripp made shadow puppets on the wall, making her laugh.

"Taking photos is helping, and having you here. Believe it or not, I am taking it all in." She smiled convincingly before snapping a photo.

"Good. That's what it's all about." Aria asked the guide to take a photo of them and Atlas, stalactites hanging like spikes around them, stalagmites growing up from the cave floor, and their shadows on the wall. Upon exiting the cave, they handed their helmets over and Aria said, "I may not be over my slight claustrophobia, but I admit I'm glad you brought me here. This was cool to see."

"Well good, because you're really going to appreciate the next stop." Tripp opened her Jeep door and she climbed in and looked at him, mouth open, about to ask where they were going when he added, "No, ma'am, it's a surprise." He chuckled as he shut the door.

"Where are we crashing tonight?" she asked, feet up on the dash and an elbow on the door.

"We're doing more than crashing," he smiled and winked, one hand resting loosely on top of the steering wheel. He didn't see her little lip bite seeing as his eyes were on the road.

"I found a perfect spot."

"You gonna tell me?"

"Nope," he teased.

"That's not fair. I let you drag me into a chopper and you won't tell me where we're staying? What if it's somewhere I don't wanna stay?" A playful smirk coaxed him to tease even further.

"You haven't been picky about accommodation thus far. And, technically, I didn't drag you onto that chopper."

"True."

"Don't you trust me?"

"I do, but your choices scare me too."

"You're one of my choices, Aria." He looked over at her, one hand on the wheel and a sultry look in his eyes as he took her hand. She held his gaze a moment before his attention went back to the road. He wasn't one for blatant eye contact like that, so when he did make the effort, it was a turn-on. Her heart would drop to the pit of her stomach every time. She had no words, just a shy smile.

"An R.V. park? We don't have an—" Her words dropped off when she saw the pioneer-style covered wagons. She whipped her head to ask him, "Is that where we're staying?"

He nodded. "Is this okay? I know it's not a hammock hanging off of a cliff but..." He shrugged sarcastically.

"Yes! I've been wanting to go glamping for a while. These look so cool." She was so excited that she was the first to hop out of the Jeep.

"Ooh, they have fire pits!" She quickly grabbed her bag from the back, letting Atlas out without his leash, but Tripp caught him by the collar before he could run off.

"These places are expensive, Tripp. As cool as this is, you didn't have to spring for it on my account."

"I didn't, technically. The company pays for our lodging."

"Oh! Well, in that case, if they're okay with it then I am too."

"I checked with my boss on the phone yesterday to make sure." They carried their bags to the little office building to check in then found their wagon. As soon as Aria's bag clunked down, she held her arms out to her sides and flopped backward onto the bed. Her hair sprawled out all around her head.

"Is it comfy?" he asked, unclipping Atlas's leash.

"Why don't you come feel for yourself?" Her mischievous grin was too tempting to pass up. He tucked his chin with a laugh before joining her. A flop onto his stomach made the bed bounce and made her giggle as he rolled onto his back and up on his elbows. She scooched toward him and took his stubbled face in her hands, taking no time to lock lips.

"Mmm, the only thing that could make this night better would be champagne and s'mores," she said, nose to nose.

He pointed to a small stand where a champagne bottle jutted

out of a metal bucket of ice next to a gift basket brimming with all the s'mores fixings.

"Aww, let's go out to the fire!" She slid herself off the bed feet first just as he was about to kiss her again. Shaking his head laughing, he followed her, but as she grabbed the bucket and basket, he politely took the bucket from her and set it back down.

"Let's save that for later," he said, a hand on the small of her back.

"Ooh, okay." She fisted his shirt, pulling him in for that kiss before heading out to the fire. He pulled her chair next to his and fetched poker sticks from a rack. Roasting marshmallows and making s'mores, cuddled up next to each other, was what life was all about. Sharing simple, relaxing moments was just as important as the fun and adventure. The scent of her perfume was stronger than the bonfire smoke at times when the breeze blew the smoke in the opposite direction. He pulled her onto his lap and watched the crackling flame, embers floating from the fire in the pit and the fire he set within her. He'd get a whiff of her vanilla scent and would close his eyes, inhaling a deep breath. She'd feel his chest rise and fall, her cheek snuggled against his neck, his arm tight around her. When the sun sank low, the air temperature dropped quickly, causing summer to feel like fall within minutes. He covered his snug t-shirt with a hoodie after handing her sweatshirt to her and he felt so cozy as she snuggled to him. His fingers would tease strands of her hair around her face and his lips would softly and subtly dance with hers. She reached beneath his hoodie, hand running up under his t-shirt, feeling his muscular frame as his warm flesh heated her hand. Their kisses turned heated, her face feeling warmer than the heat from the fire. She could only take so much cuddling though before wanting more from him. Standing, she reached for his hand. The look she gave him signaled for him to take the lead back into the wagon, Atlas remaining on the tie-out, comfortable near the fire.

"I kinda wish there weren't other campers around," Aria said, pulling Tripp's hoodie off over his head as soon as they were inside. He grinned, already aware of the reason, but asked why anyway.

"Because we could stay right out by the fire on a blanket." Removing her hair clip, she shook her hair down, letting it fall against her back.

His voice a lower tone and volume than it was moments earlier, he asked, "Yeah?" He pulled her hoodie off, her shirt coming off with it. His smile warmed her insides.

"Yeah." Wearing just a bra and jeans, she pulled his t-shirt up and he flung it to the floor before unfastening her jeans. Her hand dove down the front of his joggers and his brows rose as her lips smashed with his. She couldn't get his joggers pulled down fast enough. He couldn't unhook her bra fast enough either.

Their pulses were racing as he held her face in his hands, her fingertips digging into his back. The building heat was too much to be extinguished by the chilly night air. His tongue traced his bottom lip as she sat on the bed's edge and leaned back. He pulled her jeans off then took his time removing her panties, kissing a trail down her abdomen. He was lighting a fire within her hotter than the mid-day desert heat and a heated blush stained her cheeks once again. He crawled on top of her after stripping himself of his boxer briefs, the subtle weight of his body pressing into the mattress around her, sinking her more comfortably into its embrace. His espresso eyes dilated as he stared into hers and they explored each other's bodies, interpreting their body language like textured topography maps. His fingertips skated slowly over her mountainous chest, down to her heated valley, feeling her pooled waters. If he planned to drive her insane, it was working.

Her legs spread apart, allowing him to position himself just right and burrow slowly and deeply within her. Her back arched and her body tensed with a thrust from his hips. Sparks flew and her heart pounded wildly as the inferno within her blazed into a raging wildfire. Her hand tangled in his hair, giving it a yank as she nibbled his bottom lip.

"Mmm..." He let out a lingering groan. Taking hold of his shoulders, she'd lift a little with each time he thrust, sending a jolt of ecstasy through her that had her begging for more. Moans had to have been heard from outside their wagon. Having her naked skin flush against his...there was nothing on Earth better than this.

Mile Marker 15: Flagstaff

"Any specific stops planned for Flagstaff?" Aria asked, looking up places to eat nearby on her phone as they were about to enter town.

"Nah. If you find somewhere you wanna stop, just holler. Oh! There's the extreme adventure course!"

"Or...ancient lava tubes, whatever that is." She scrolled her screen, her attempt to avoid heights not going unnoticed by a snickering Tripp.

"Boutique shops?"

"We could do that." That seemed to have her attention.

He nodded.

"Ooh, there's a candy shop! Let's take a break from all the dirt. I can still taste it from the dunes." She rubbed her front teeth with her finger before running her tongue along them.

"Me too." He laughed. "Let's get all hyped up in a sugary bliss."

"I love it! There's a train that runs through here?" she asked, noticing a set of railroad tracks ahead that they were about to cross.

"I think it's a day trip and they go to the canyon and loop back around."

"Well, we've already seen all of that."

"Let's just make this stop a short one. We can hit some shops and eat, then continue," Tripp suggested, driving by the museum.

"Sounds good. I don't feel like getting dirty again anytime soon."

"No?" he asked, pulling into a parking spot along the shops. When she turned to look at him, he was smirking.

"That depends."

"Oh? On what?" His brow raised and he put the Jeep in park.

"On what kind of dirty you meant." Her fingers ran along the hem of his t-shirt sleeve, sliding underneath.

"Is that so?" Now both brows raised as he leaned in toward her over the console as he unbuckled.

"Tripp...I'm surprised." She gasped, her hand upon her chest dramatically, barely managing to maintain a straight face. He laughed, adjusting his ball cap backward before stealing a kiss—a good one too. She felt herself melting, weak with his touch as he took the side of her face in his hand. Their lips parted slowly, her eyes still closed a moment longer in an effort to savor the moment.

"Let's go shoppin'," Tripp said, exiting the Jeep with Atlas hot on his heels.

"I'm perfectly okay with continuing what we just had going." Aria exited the Jeep before Tripp could open her door.

"Well, I guess there'll have to be another surprise later then." He seemed on a mission as he stepped up onto the sidewalk.

"Later, huh? You're a tease." She smiled excitedly, a lip bite added as she joined him on the sidewalk, taking his hand.

He grinned. "Yep. Right now, I want some ice cream." Tripp glanced down at Atlas on the leash next to him, who barked. "He agrees."

"I see. So, you both want to spoil your appetite for lunch?"

"We're adults so there are no such rules."

"I see. Majority rules so ice cream it is." Aria hooked arms with Tripp, strolling down the sidewalk and pointing out shops she wanted to check out during their Flagstaff in-town excursion.

Ice cream didn't cool off Aria's feverish need for Tripp, as she couldn't help but stare at him. The way his arm muscles would flex with each turn of the steering wheel, his curls resting on the back of his neck, his strong jawline, and how badly she wanted to feel his scruff...it was all too much. She had no idea what song was even playing on the radio because all she could hear were the sexual thoughts running through her head.

"Pull over," Aria blurted.

"What? Why?" He turned to her, a concerned look on his face.

"Please? I don't want you swerving all over the road." She sounded urgent.

"Okay." He slowed the Jeep and pulled over onto the shoulder of the road as Aria unbuckled and began groping him, leaning over across the console.

The grin on his face spread wide as she bit his lip roughly, unbuckling him, and crawling over to his lap. He moved his seat back and gripped her thigh as she straddled him. As she kissed her way down his neck with a hand up his shirt, he tipped his head back against the headrest.

"What's gotten into you all of a sudden?" he asked, still grinning as he grabbed her ass cheeks under the edge of her skirt.

"Are you complaining?" she whispered, breathy.

"Hell no." His lips smashed into hers as she released him from his pants that he barely got slid down enough before she took him in. The horn honked once as her ass hit it, making them laugh but not stopping them.

Having released her sexual energy after a thirty-minute Jeep-rocking roadside fantasy was executed, they put themselves back together and continued on their way.

Mile Marker 16: Meteor Crater

A detour to Meteor Crater produced fascinating photos. They used themselves in a few of them to show size comparison to the crater. The dark, dusty path to and from the crater caused a desperate need to shower. Needing to add a few vacation rental homes to the travel blog, and one with a washer, they found a quiet place entering Phoenix. The cute stucco home had traditional arched doorways and a property full of cacti. Before unloading their bags, Tripp broke off a piece from a cactus.

"Will you get in trouble for that?" Aria looked around, noticing a camera mounted on the front of the house.

"Nah. Have you ever drank from a cactus?"

"Uh...no, I can't say I have." She walked over to Tripp in the front yard while Atlas wandered around, sniffing everything. Tripp handed her the piece he broke off and nodded for her to try it. She took it and hesitated for a moment, looking at it with a scrunched nose.

"It's mainly water so there isn't much of a taste." He chuckled, sucking liquid from another chunk he broke off. He waited patiently, staring her down as she cautiously tasted the cacti liquid.

"Okay, it's not bad. If I were dehydrating like a raisin out in the desert, I'd drink it." She shrugged, making him laugh. They took their bags inside, and after a quick trip to a local grocery store while laundry was running, used the charcoal grill out back to cook dinner.

"I didn't know you could cook so well." She hid a mouthful with her hand as she spoke.

"Well, not to sound cocky or anything, but now ya know." He chuckled. "I like to cook during the time when I'm home and not traveling. I've learned a few things on the road. I've had to improvise here and there."

"It's another talent you've surprised me with." Her green eyes looked up at him as she swallowed and smiled mischievously. "This tastes better than just improvising."

"Thanks. So, I've impressed you?"

"Very much."

"There's a lot you don't know about me yet."

"I'm looking forward to learning what I don't yet know." She shot him a wink with that sly smile, making him laugh.

A relaxing cuddle by the fire outside after dark was a much-needed end to the day. They didn't bother cleaning up after dinner, they just looked forward to being in each other's arms.

"I think I'm gonna go get out of these jeans and take a shower." Aria stood from sitting on Tripp's lap and turned to see his slow-spreading smile. She found it to be quite teasing.

"Yeah, we should probably wash this smoke from our hair. I'll be sneezing all night." He stood and followed her into the house, contemplating joining her in the shower. He wasn't too shy to make that bold of a move anymore, was he? To walk in and strip down, her naked body on display beneath the water falling upon her supple skin? He insisted she shower first so the thought would remain a fantasy for now. She came out of the bathroom wearing a crop-top tank and pj shorts that may have just barely covered her butt cheeks and towel dried her hair. He had tidied up the mess he had made when he hauled everything in earlier and cleaned up the kitchen and was leaning over his bag, pulling out a pair of shorts.

Looking up, he took a double take. He couldn't help but stare at her. He realized he was staring as he watched her tuck her hair behind her ear. Those pretty irises of his looked away quickly, interrupting his own trance.

"Shower's yours." Her bare feet barely made a sound as she walked toward him and whipped her towel playfully at his ass as she walked by. A wide, white smile from him as his eyes followed her forced her to shy hers away as she continued to her room. About ten minutes later, she heard him get out of the shower and tell Atlas to go to bed with a finger snap. She assumed he was headed to bed in the second bedroom, so as she pulled the covers back on the bed she hollered, "Goodnight, Tripp!"

"Going to sleep already?" he asked, suddenly leaning in her bedroom doorway, startling her. He chuckled. "Sorry." His chest was still damp and he stood in only shorts. She chucked a pillow at him but he caught it and walked it back to her. "You wanna finish what we started?"

"Good thing I'm not that tired yet," she said with a smirk as she snatched the pillow back. His two-day rogue stubble had been freshly shaved in all the right places, leaving perfection, his wet hair instantly curly already. She couldn't break eye contact with him as he closed the gap between them. Her heart began racing and her cheeks felt flushed as he took her by the waist.

"What do you think about sharing a room tonight?" he asked.

"I think I'd be more than okay with that." She laughed, seeing no point in concealing her excitement. "You weren't really going to sleep in the other room, were you?" Her arms wrapped up around his neck, her fingers playing with his curls. He wore a mischievous smile as she pulled him down to her for his lips to meet hers.

"Not a chance," he growled in her ear, sending a shiver up her spine. She was losing herself in this man she had quickly gotten to know.

Mile Marker 17: Phoenix

"Why did we have to get up so early?" Aria yawned and stretched her arms into the air, makeup bag in hand as she came out of the bathroom minutes after their shower... together. Tripp was carrying their bags out the front door, Atlas on his heels, but he stopped in the doorway to answer her.

"I have a surprise for you." That mischievous smirk worried her a bit as he flipped his sunglasses down to his eyes and continued to the Jeep.

"Oh no," she mumbled as she slipped on her not-so-white anymore canvas shoes. She took a sweep of the place, making sure they wouldn't be leaving anything behind.

Once they had pulled away from the house, he asked, "Didn't that shower wake you up?"

With a giggle, she said, "It did. I think I may be worn out again though." She could see in her peripheral vision that he was grinning ear to ear. He reached over, his fingers teasing the exposed flesh of her thigh. She loved his hands on her. They shared a special connection, a mutual unspoken respect. There was no tension between them to be alleviated. He smelled of that fresh-after-a-rainstorm scent; a breath of fresh air.

"Can we stop for coffee?" she asked, intertwining her fingers with his on her thigh.

"There'll be coffee where we're going."

"Is that so?"

"Absolutely. Breakfast too."

Suddenly she wasn't as nervous. "You're really not going to tell me where we're going?"

"Into Phoenix."

"Yeah, but what are we doing? What's the plan?"

His head tilted as he looked over at her briefly, not answering.

"Tripp."

"Hmm?" His attention was back on the road ahead, his knee steering the wheel as he put his hair into a messy bun.

"I'm not gonna like it, am I?" She twisted in her seat, facing him, the nervousness rushing back.

He inhaled a deep breath and said, "We can stop now for coffee too if you want."

"Topic deflector. You're avoiding my question."

"Mmmm, more than you know."

"I'm assuming I won't be a fan of what you have planned then. How are you going to terrify me now?" Her head tilted sideways and she cracked a half-smile.

"You're adorable, you know that?"

"Now you're using flattery in hopes I'll stop asking."

"Pretty much. You are adorable though." He nodded, then gave Atlas's head a stratchin' above the console. She sat with her back against the seat, biting the inside of her lip and brainstorming the ways he could be trying to trick her into facing more fears.

"I'll stop asking if you buy me a latte."

"Deal." He made a quick turn into a coffee shop parking lot.

She sipped that latte with her coral-painted toes up on the dash, him watching her as she watched the reflection of a helicopter and clouds in the windshield as they drove.

"Tripp! Look!" Aria pointed out the open Jeep window as they turned off from the main road.

"Hey, look at that. We didn't miss all the balloons after all." He turned his head, not able to conceal a smirk.

"Think we can get a few photos while we're passing through? Since we're looping back toward Florida, we won't be passing by here again."

"Sure."

Amongst a field of full parking, they managed to find an empty parking space. She grabbed the camera bag and Tripp clipped Atlas's leash onto his collar. There were hot air balloons of all colors and designs, acres of them. Aria snapped photos from a distance then, walking between them, Tripp and Atlas walking with her, took in the sights.

"They're so colorful!"

"They are. I know your heart's colorful language and it speaks beautiful words."

"Oh, Tripp. You're such a romantic." She squeezed his arm. "I think I've probably taken enough photos." She began to put the camera away but he touched her hand.

"Wait. You didn't take any of being inside a basket. Maybe one looking up would be a cool view. We need a selfie inside one anyway for your scrapbook. They're tied down."

She hesitated then said, "Okay, I guess we could do that."

They stepped into one; the most unique one. It had the pattern of a vintage map with the countries shaded in hues of blue. The swooshing of a sudden flame seemed much louder inside the balloon than outside and a gentleman came over to their basket. Tripp spoke briefly with him in a quiet tone and Aria was struggling to hear the conversation as loud swooshes of air were keeping balloons afloat.

"These still rock a bit even being staked down," she sat on the basket floor, looking up into the balloon, taking pics after the guy took their photo together.

"Yeah, they just catch air," Tripp said passively as he took a picnic basket from the guy and shut the basket door before the basket was de-staked and left the ground. Tripp laid out a picnic blanket that was folded on top of the basket. He rushed to unpack the basket of goodies that came with the balloon flight package, champagne included for morning mimosas. He stood when she stood, worried about what her reaction would be now that they were about thirty feet off the ground or more. She was still snapping photos, dozens of other balloons in the air lifting off with them. It took her a moment to realize all of the balloons were floating together in the air. The camera slipped from her grip but the strap around her neck caught it as it slapped against her chest. He was thinking *oh shit, she's going to flip out,* so he came up behind her and wrapped his arms around her. She turned to him with huge eyes and froze as her breathing became panicked.

"It's okay, Aria," he said, tightening his hold around her.

"We're in the air!" she screeched.

"I know. I know. It's okay." He took the camera strap off her neck and set it down before wrapping his arms around her again.

"Tripp! What the—" Her voice was trembling in time with the rest of her body. She buried her face in his chest, eyes squinted shut tight. He rubbed her back up and down and said, "I knew you'd say no if I asked to take a flight."

"Of course I would've said no!"

"What have you got to lose?"

"My life."

"Besides that?" He chuckled after pausing and staring a moment at her huge scared eyes, trying to make her laugh.

"Tripp," she pouted.

"I know you're scared, but I just want you to live life, to conquer your fears, and to be able to say 'I did that'."

"I just wanna live, Tripp! Literally!" She felt as though her heart was about to leap out of her chest, free-falling into the canyon.

He laughed. "I'm right here. Have I let any harm come to you yet?"

She shook her head no, her forehead against his peck.

"Look. We can sit on this blanket and enjoy breakfast. There are even mimosas. Might relax ya. You did once tell me to push you to help you conquer fears...right? Unless—"

She looked up at him.

"I did say that, unfortunately. I'm currently regretting it too. You have a death wish, don't you?" she choked out the words, fear strangling her from within her throat.

"What? Don't be silly. Atlas is even enjoying himself," Tripp looked down at the dog, who was lying on the blanket. She inhaled deeply, the fear not having left her eyes yet. A breeze blew her hair across her face and he pushed it back behind her shoulder, his brown eyes staring back at her. She held his wrists as he cradled her face in his hands and pressed his lips to hers. When her world stopped spinning, he was holding on to her protectively. Perhaps he was the reason she felt grounded again. Suddenly, she felt safer and the kiss he left on her forehead secured that feeling of trust in him. *He* was her safe haven no matter where they were or what they were doing, and he had proved it, over and over again, even if she was terrified at first. The experiences themselves weren't regrettable.

"Let's pop open this champagne," he said excitedly, coaxing a smile from her.

"How high is this thing going to float?" she asked, holding both glasses while he popped the cork and champagne bubbled down the bottle. He shrugged when he said, "I can slow it down, then it won't go much higher." He poured their drinks and corked the bottle before pulling the cord to open the valve, releasing a little hot air to slow its ascent.

"How'd you know how to do that," she asked with a cheers bump to his glass. They took a sip before he answered, her face feeling fizz from the champagne before her lips did.

"I've done this before. Well, not the romantic picnic, but the balloon thing. It wasn't a balloon festival like this, but I took a privately owned one up to take some scenic photos."

"Atlas too?" she looked at the dog licking the spilled champagne soaking into the blanket.

"Yep."

"So that's why he isn't freaking out. I should've known."

He laughed. "Last time we were in New Mexico though, it was in October, so not quite as hot. He looked over the side the whole time."

"I suppose the scenery isn't much different."

"Except here we have a great view of the Grand Canyon and I have someone special to share it with." He pointed, urging her to look, but she was afraid to tip the basket if she moved. He laughed at her stubborn attempt to not rock them off balance.

"Okay, you step forward and I'll step back at the same time."

She looked at him a moment, unsure that plan would work, but then stood as he did, trusting him. With a nod from him, they stepped apart at the same time. Still afraid to get too close to the side, she looked out over the desert landscape.

"Oh wow...this is..."

"Cool, right?"

"Really cool." She turned to him, smiling, drink in hand, high on adrenaline. He had Atlas sit next to him on his side of the basket before he grabbed the camera and took a photo of her looking out at the canyon. He carefully stepped up behind her and kissed her shoulder, handing her the camera and taking her glass from her hand before wrapping an arm around the front of her. With no ground below in sight, only off in the distance, he felt as though he was soaring above the endless Earth with no future destination except with her.

"For a minute I forgot all about taking photos." She snapped a few then held on to his arm.

"It's good to be caught up in the moment. The view is just too amazing to pass up a photo of though."

"It is, isn't it?" she snapped a few more, adjusting settings.

"It really is," he agreed, looking at her, taking in her beauty. She turned to him, wrapping her arms around him, camera strapped around her neck, her attention focused on him and this moment rather than her fear, before capturing his lips with hers. He had her on a high that she didn't want to come down from, free-falling...in love.

"I'm on cloud nine with you, Tripp."

"I was hoping so."

The weather was perfect for breakfast in the sky and the scenery was breathtaking. The company was perfect too.

Mile Marker 18: Tucson

Aria took the reins for a while in the driver seat. Tripp's head was leaned back onto the headrest, his dark lashes resting against his cheeks. He was gorgeous and had a soul to match. She'd look over at him often, watching him sleep. He tipped over further against the door, arms crossed against his chest, comfortably situated. She was starting to daydream, wanting to be in constant contact with his body. The thought of reaching over to touch him through those joggers crossed her mind but she didn't want to wake him until they were close to their destination.

An impromptu horseback ride on a beaten trail that took them through desert canyons somewhere between Phoenix and Tucson was more Aria's speed. She had found something adventurous that she was more comfortable doing than Tripp was. Atlas trotted alongside the horses as if he were one of them. That short five-mile walk got Tripp's heart racing faster than any other adventure they had been on. Aria couldn't help but let out a little laugh when Tripp shouted at his horse to slow down.

"I'm understanding your discomfort in trying new adventures, Aria."

"You don't like horses?" she snickered.

"I'm just not familiar with them. I rode once as a kid."

"A pony ride at the fair doesn't count, Tripp."

"How'd you know?" he adjusted his butt in the saddle.

She laughed. "Wanna make 'em run?"

"No!" His eyes were huge.

"I'm certain those thighs of yours can hold on well enough."

"Nope, I'm good. I apologize by the way."

"For what?"

"For making you feel uncomfortable at any point on this trip."

She turned her head to laugh.

"It's okay. I should slap your horse's ass though to make you feel as scared as I've been."

"I'd deserve that."

"You do. But I won't do it."

"Oh, thank God." He sighed with relief. "You sure? Because you're grinning. I see you biting your cheek." He let his horse slow just enough to ensure his horse's rear was out of Aria's reach. She looked back at him and laughed.

"These animals have so much power, it's scary. They're unpredictable."

"Gravity isn't?" She steered her horse around a downed branch.

"Okay, you have a point. Actually, no. Gravity is pretty predictable. Can be scary too." His horse stepped over the branch.

"Hmmm horses with gravity factored in *are* scary." She giggled at her own sarcasm. "I'd love just enough land to have a horse someday."

"Or close enough to ride someone else's?"

"What?" she looked back at him, confused.

He caught back up to her.

"Cheaper that way." He laughed. "I'm buying an acre. Just have to sign the papers."

"Really? Where?"

"Back home."

"Which is where, exactly?"

"North of Pensacola."

She smiled wide.

"What?" he asked, adjusting his shades on his face.

"I'm from that area."

"Originally or...?"

"Yes and that's where I live."

"No way!" The surprised grin on his face was a happy one.

"So, the land you bought must be near horses?"

"Yeah. The guy I work for, Jake, told me his best friend would sell me land. It's next to his riding stables. I only bought an acre so I can put a tiny house on it. I'm not home enough to rent or have a big house to take care of."

"Traveling makes for a better life anyway so that sounds perfect."

"Exactly. I rather be traveling than be stuck in one spot for too long at a time. I don't have to get *such* a tiny house though if I had a roommate." He shot her a high brow. "I mean, you rent, right?"

"I do. I don't have a roommate anymore either and my rent is about to go up. I was planning to scout new places when I get back from vacation."

"Or..." He stared at her, waiting for a reply.

"Or...?" She stared back.

"Or we can be roommates."

"Really? You'd wanna live with me after you've put up with me this whole trip?"

He shrugged and said, "Why not? We get along great."

She looked away, trying to hide her excitement before putting on her less excited face.

"It's a thought. I wanted to put the offer out there." His chin tipped down a moment, preparing for disappointment before looking away.

"I like the idea."

His chin shot up and his eyes dashed to meet hers.

"You do?"

"Yeah, I do. Are you asking me to move in with you, Tripp?"

Those white teeth flashed as he nodded and said, "Yeah, I am."

"Then yes. So, when you pick out the house, let me know how much I'd owe you each month."

"Well, since it was in my plans already, why don't you help me pick the house out and we call it even?"

"What do you mean? Of course, I'd pay rent. Don't be silly."

"I'm not asking you to pay rent."

"Don't be ridiculous. I couldn't...I wouldn't feel right living there without pitching in."

"Fine. Electricity and water then."

"That's not fair. That's not nearly as much as rent would be."

"Then it looks like you'll have to keep scouting for something more expensive." He wore a serious face but couldn't contain it when her jaw dropped at his audacity. He busted out an echoing laugh.

"Fine. Utilities it is. Not sure I could find a place next to horses nor a roommate as cool anyway." She turned her head away, nose in the air in a false show of indifference.

"That's what I thought," he mumbled.

"Thanks for letting me take the lead on this adventure." Aria pulled her ball cap down to better shield her eyes from the blazing evening sun.

Tripp smiled, shaking his head. "Sure."

"I bet you won't wanna let me drive again though, huh?" Her wide smile was playful.

His laugh echoed off the orange canyon walls.

"Where to next?" she asked as she noticed Tripp was looking a bit worn out.

"Slumberland."

Mile Marker 19: Watch Your Step

B efore leaving the gas station, Aria took Atlas to a designated doggy area while Tripp freshened the ice in the cooler and poured a bowl of water for Atlas at the Jeep. He attached the spare gas can to the back side window. Atlas sniffed around and did his business, but on his trot back to Aria, stopped dead in his tracks not far from her. His head lowered slowly and his ears pinned back, a front leg picked up. She clapped her leg and took a step, beginning to turn around, but Atlas barked. Aria turned back in his direction to call him.

"You find pickers, buddy?" Aria took a step forward but Atlas barked at her aggressively and kept growling. She stopped, hands on her hips and brows furrowed.

"Atlas? What's wrong?" She was surprised at his otherwise calm behavior.

"What's he doing?" Tripp wiped his wet hands on his khaki cargo shorts, walking toward them.

"I don't know. He's acting weird. Atl—" She was interrupted by another bark.

"He's trying to warn us about som"—he paused and cocked his head, listening—"You hear that?"

"Hear what?" she whispered.

He held his finger to his lips, listening, about five steps behind her.

"He doesn't want us going any closer to him for some reason." Her words trailed off as she heard a hiss and rattle.

"Shit! Where is it?" Tripp asked quietly, looking around from where he stood. Little patches of grassy weeds were all that stood between them and Atlas. There was movement behind a decent-sized patch and Atlas growled and barked, hopping backward a step.

"Aria, don't move." Tripp took a slow step forward toward her, then another and put his hand on her shoulder.

"Is that a—"

"Rattler. Yep. Don't move," he whispered back, widened eyes locked on the snake, feet frozen in place as he quickly thought of a plan to detour the rattler.

Atlas stepped sideways, about to go around to join Tripp and Aria, when the snake struck at the dog, frightened by sudden movement, luckily missing him. Atlas started jumping around and barking, attempting to distract the snake from the couple, then making his way over to Tripp, who was calling his name in an effort to get him to leave the snake alone. When Atlas got close to Aria, the snake slithered about a foot or more closer before stopping, half coiled and tail rattling, its head held up a good foot height off the ground. As it was about to strike in their direction to warn them away from its resting place, Tripp quickly stepped in front of Aria, blocking her, and chucked his knife at the snake. It hit the snake behind the head, pinning it into the clay ground. The rattle slowed and Tripp crept up on it. The sharp blade almost took the snake's head clean off.

"Just reflexes, I guess." He grabbed his knife and stepped on the snake to pull the knife out of it. The dead animal flopped to the ground, lifeless. Aria stood, frozen, fingers to her mouth and her eyes wide. Tripp walked toward her, paying attention to wiping snake blood onto his shorts from the blade. When he looked up at her, he saw how freaked out she was. He folded the knife and stuck it into his pocket before taking her by the shoulders, bending to her level, and looking her in her panicked eyes.

"Aria? You okay?"

She nodded.

"It's okay. It's okay. It's dead, we're safe now. I feel bad killing it but it was the safest option with Atlas running around out here."

"That was close. This could've been really bad. There isn't a hospital for miles."

"It's ok. Atlas warned us in time."

"You...you saved us, Tripp. Again." She wrapped her arms around him, hands on his back, cheek flush to his chest. He hugged her, resting his chin on her head.

"This was my fault," he admitted. She pulled away just enough to look up at him.

"What are you talking about?"

"You were walking my dog."

"So?"

"So, that's why you were near that snake."

"I'm glad Atlas sensed danger and I'm thankful you were quick with that knife. Nice aim, by the way."

He chuckled. "Thanks. It was wrong place, wrong time there for a few heart-racing moments."

"It sure as hell was. I was actually scared. You were in the right place at the right time. Like always. I'm so glad I bought you that knife."

He gave her a fiery kiss, then walked with her toward the Jeep, Atlas on their heels. Atlas received a bag of beef jerky for his heroic efforts and thank you hugs before loading up.

"Me too. Let's get outta here. I got a knife to clean."

Mile Marker 20: White Sands & San Antonio

A detour to White Sands in New Mexico was worth the extra time. That sugar-white sand was like nothing they had seen in weeks. It was magical, absolutely remarkable. The ripples across the sand's surface ran parallel to the line of white clouds in the sky. The most breathtaking photos were those taken of the two of them. The sparked creativity of the photo opportunities led to memorable treasures behind the lens. The blue sky and perfect weather allowed for photo clarity. Her flowy chiffon white dress caught the breeze and matched perfectly with his white t-shirt. His dark hair and black jogger pants were a perfect contrast. The sand was warm between their bare toes. A set timer was helpful with taking couples photos; holding hands walking toward and away from the camera, him lifting her into the air, and a photo-bomb shot of them laughing as Atlas ran at the camera, lips and ears flapping and drool flying as he chased a bird. Priceless. Their love was blossoming and the proof was in the photos; her vision of their future collaging together as a reality.

The next stop was San Antonio. A visit to The Alamo taught them some interesting history and they met a local there who pointed them in the direction of a barbecue competition taking place in town that couldn't be passed up. Multicolored tents provided much-needed shade for the Texas grill masters. There were fire pits, grills, roaster cookers, and smokers. The seasoning and sauce choices were plentiful and were shelved according to spice level. There were brands and flavor combinations that they had never heard of and a spice level chart was plastered on a wooden sign between tents.

"Wow, where do we even start?" Aria scooped Tripp's arm with hers as they entered the roped off event.

"I didn't realize how hungry I was. I say we try a little of everything," Tripp suggested.

"I'm game."

"How hot you like it?" Tripp asked, bumping elbows with her. She laughed when he winked.

They stepped up to the first tent.

"Smells delicious," she mumbled to Tripp before their turn to order. Drool was dripping from Atlas's mouth.

"Sure does. Let's do a sampler. A little of everything ya got, please."

"Sure. Ya like it spicy?" the cook asked Aria, who tucked her hair behind her ear and looked up at him with shy eyes.

"Yes, sir. Oh! You meant the wings? Yeah, sure."

Tripp busted out a loud, uncontrollable laugh and rubbed her back, easing her embarrassment.

Picnic tables had been set up beneath colorful triangle sunshades, the perfect spot to sit and enjoy the food.

"You have a little something." She pointed at his mustache.

"Where? Here?" He'd touch a spot and she'd shake her head no. Then another spot and she shook her head again. She walked over to his side of the picnic table and sat next to him. She tipped his chin toward her and kissed him, making sure to get the barbecue sauce. By the fifth tent, they had sampled enough to be completely stuffed and know what they were looking for to take home with them, so Tripp shopped seasonings at a vendor booth.

"So many choices." Tripp read labels as he picked out a few.

"Are you going to become a grill master now?" she asked sarcastically.

"I don't know about that, but I've been inspired." He raised his brows a quick shot and flipped a seasoning jar in the air, smoothly catching it after a few rotations.

"Hey, you wanna do some shooting tonight?"

"Shooting? As in guns?"

"Yeah." He shrugged, picking out a sauce and handing the vendor cash.

"Sure. I don't know much about guns though, to be honest." She took the sauce bottle from him, checking out the label.

"I can teach you if you want. The place we're staying at tonight has a huge dirt field behind it with mounds we can shoot into. That's what drew my attention to that accommodation."

"They have guns and equipment too?"

"I have my handgun and ammo. I'll stop and buy ear protection for us."

"You've had a gun in the Jeep this whole time?"

"Yeah, of course. Does that freak you out?" He wrinkled a brow, hoping this wouldn't deter her decision to keep traveling with him.

"No, I mean, I'm glad I wasn't aware of it until I got to know you though. Trust might have been more of an issue."

He chuckled. "I understand that. I'm just used to carrying, that's all. I'm usually traveling alone so it's safer to carry."

"Even though my car broke down, I'm the hitchhiker, so good thing you can trust me too," she bantered.

"Exactly." He laughed.

After buying needed items at a sporting goods store downtown, they settled into their rental for the evening. Before sundown, Tripp shut Atlas in the house and he and Aria headed out back to the make-shift berm range on the property. Tripp showed Aria how to load the gun after he dropped the magazine and cleared the chamber, teaching her how to properly load it herself. She held it, pointed it down and away from their bodies until in position, then keeping the business end aimed down range, she aimed at the target that was stapled to the board within the berm.

"Have you been shooting before?" he asked, securing his ear protection.

"I've only fired a gun once."

"Did it go well? You seem to know what you're doing," he asked. "The safety is on, by the way."

"Well, I didn't shoot anyone if that's what you mean." She laughed.

"Okay, well that's good." He laughed, shaking his head at her vague sarcasm. He stood behind her, chin above her shoulder, and showed her how to correctly aim at the target by guiding her arms and stance. She paid more attention to how his touch felt than what he was instructing. Her heart was racing, just as it always did when he was this close to her.

"Whenever you're ready, exhale and go for it. Shoot all the rounds." He stepped back.

She exhaled fully then shot until the magazine was empty.

"Bullseye!" Tripp shouted excitedly. She set the gun down and tried to focus her eyes on the target before facing him.

"Really? I hit the target?"

"Hell yeah you did! You didn't just hit the target, I bet that first fire was a bullseye shot." He made sure the firearm was empty and set it in its case before waving for her to walk with him to take a closer look. He reached the target before her and pointed at the hole almost dead center, the others close.

"Wow! You killed it, Aria! Great job!"

She squealed with excitement.

"I'm proud of you. You should be proud too." He scooped her up in a hug and spun her around, her feet off the ground.

"Wanna quit while you're ahead?" he asked with a smirk.

"What? No way!"

"If it's beginner's luck, I don't want you feeling disappointed later." He teased, bumping her elbow with his as they walked back, side-by-side.

"Nice try. There's no way I'm quitting this early. You're just worried I'm gonna show you up."

"What? No way."

"Let's see whatcha got then." She shoved him lightly then ran, almost knocking him off balance. He ran to catch up with her, but beat her back to where the gun was laying on a handmade podium in its case. He reloaded the magazine and chambered a round.

"Fun fact: most women are better shots than men." She said, standing behind him, hands on her hips.

"Actually, that's true." He agreed with a smirk and nodded, pointing the gun down range. The gun fired and he shouted, throwing his fist in the air.

"Nuh uh." Her hands were on her hips and she shifted her weight to one side. He fired off the rest of the rounds.

"Are you competitive?" he asked, the biggest grin on his face.

"I didn't think so, but this is fun. I didn't expect there to be competition to worry about."

"Oh! Is that right? So, you see me as competition? Well, I've had some training and well...you're a woman, so it makes sense we're pretty good."

"Thanks. I wanna see where that shot hit." She waited for him to set the empty gun back into the case then took him by the hand as they walked out to the target. Her bullet hole was twice as wide as before and there were no other holes in the target. He smiled a bright wide smile, making her laugh.

"Damn, you *are* good! That's hot!" She grabbed the front of his t-shirt and pulled him to her for a kiss. His brows rose and she purposely knocked his hat off onto the ground, her arms wrapping around his neck. Her lips were tingling and the tingle radiated throughout her body; it did every time they kissed. She could feel her body temperature rising quickly. Sinking into him, he made her melt, his curls tickling her arm behind his neck. His lips pulled away from hers reluctantly. She looked so beautiful, her face glowing in the light of the sinking sun. He couldn't help but stare at her in the glow of the golden hour.

"Are you ready to take this inside?" she asked, biting her bottom lip.

"Oh, you have no idea. You done shooting for now?"

"We're both equally good, which would make it boring to continue...this competition anyway."

"Mmm, challenge accepted. I prefer your idea."

She could feel the rumble of his words on her neck and looked down at the joggers he wore before replying with batting eyes, "I can tell." Her gaze met his before she grabbed his shirt and pulled him in for another lip smashing, tongue twisting competition. He took her hand and led her toward the house, his curly locks bouncing against the back of his neck with each step, all the way to the back yard. He stopped suddenly and ran back, snatching the gun case at the field's edge before catching up to a giggling Aria at the back door of the house.

She stripped her clothes off, leaving a trail for him to follow. He set the gun down on the end table then quickly discarded his clothes on top of hers, bare feet following her footsteps to the bedroom. She pulled back the covers on the bed, him right behind her, enjoying the view. She took him by the shoulders and pushed him onto the bed, straddling him immediately. He scooched back, taking her with him until his head was on the pillow. Taking no time for teasing, he drove himself into her as she gripped his chest, her nails sinking in. The ends of her hair felt like silk against his skin as she tipped her head back. Her hips swirled slowly, once, twice, grinding him deeper and making his eyes roll back. She reached back and grabbed his thigh.

"My God, you feel so good," she whispered in his ear as he sat up and kissed the delicate skin of her neck.

"Mmm, you feel amazing," he murmured, his lips moving to hers, his tongue slipping back into her mouth. Every time he'd do that, butterflies fluttered in her stomach and her hands would travel his body more aggressively. He flipped her over onto her back, taking control, then reached back and pulled the covers up over them. Her arching movements and wandering hands expressed desire for him, mirroring his desire for her. The tenderness of his touch made her close her eyes, taking it all in. She let down his hair, unraveling the curls. Their kissing became more fervent, bodies close, becoming one, and feeling the strong connection between them as if they had known each other somehow in a previous life. His lashes fluttered against hers, noses touched, his forehead pressing gently against hers as her moans began to sound less repressed. The way he fit perfectly with her, within her, how she felt with him intimately, it was all surreal. His rhythm was steady, perfect, increasing her pleasure with each wave.

Consumed by the feeling of her walls caressing his length, he kissed her senseless while plunging himself into her, making her cry out as her legs quivered and quaked. Touching his jawline, with his face against hers, she felt him smile. A few more thrusts and she felt his wave of release. He exhaled a deep breath with a groan, his gaze softening and fixating on hers as he caressed her cheek with his fingertips. She held his loose, frizzing curls back from his face and dragged gaze from his pretty brown eyes down to his needy lips as she leaned up, slowly to connect hers to his. Her hair spread out around her on the pillow when she laid back, and he lay next to her, adjusting the covers and resting with a hand behind his head. She rolled to him, a leg up over his, her palm resting between her face and his chest. The feeling of his fingers gently trailing up and down her side lulled her into a relaxed state of utter bliss. The stars seemed brighter that night as she snuggled warmly to him.

Mile Marker 21: Houston

"So, we're passing through Houston next. There's an aquarium and the space center too, if those are places you care to check out." Tripp placed his coffee cup in the console cup holder and cracked open an energy drink. Aria wasn't finished with her coffee yet so got a kick out of how much caffeine he was drinking so early.

"What were your original plans for Houston?"

"I need to meet up with Jake at the rodeo. That's where we need to take some good photos and video for the magazine, but Jake let me extend the trip time, so if you want to stop at other places, we can."

"Whatever we cross paths with is fine by me."

They ended up visiting both and spent the morning playing tourist, snorkeling with sharks, marveling at the rockets, and taking goofy pictures all over the city.

"I guess we've done passed lunchtime."

"I'm fine with just eating once today."

A billboard for a famous taco truck caught Aria's eye.

"Wanna try it?" she pointed to the sign.

"You really wanna risk that again?"

She laughed. "It'll be fine. I won't eat guacamole. Our day has gone without a hitch and I have the pills just in case."

"We don't need ya sleeping in the stands at the rodeo," he joked.

"Haha."

"If you want tacos, we'll get tacos."

"Yes, please." Her smile was wide, almost begging, and he just couldn't say no.

~

"Wow! This place is packed!" Aria spun in a circle, taking in the packed dirt parking lot for the rodeo grounds.

"Oh yeah. It's a big annual event."

"Have you ever been to this particular event before?"

"Nope. I'm looking forward to it. Jake will be here. We'll need to get good video footage and pictures for the magazine while we're here. He'll post the footage on social media after editing. Since the magazine is mainly Western themed, the rodeo will be a huge spread in this next issue." Tripp let Atlas out of the car and hooked his leash to his collar while Aria grabbed the camera bag.

"I think we can handle that. I'm excited. I've never been to a rodeo before." She flung the strap over her shoulder and shut the door before joining him at the front of the Jeep.

"Really?"

"Really."

"It'll be another first-time adventure for you then."

"One I'll remember for sure."

"The best adventures are the ones that make for interesting stories down the road. Everyone loves a good story. Hopefully the bull riders stay safe, but we kinda need a little bit of wild action too."

"Absolutely."

The rodeo was already underway by the time they made it into the arena.

"I'd like to find Jake really quick before we start with photos, unless you'd like to take some along the way. The scenery in the background is ideal." Tripp led the way through the crowd along the outdoor arena gates, Atlas leading both of them and Aria staying close.

"Sure!" She carefully removed the camera from the bag she carried cross-body and screwed the lens on, then managed to capture a few scenic shots before they ran into Jake.

He stood along a metal gate, one foot up on a rail and an arm hanging over. His dark five o'clock shadow was cut about the same style as Tripp's, but Jake's dark hair was much shorter. It was more than long enough on top to run fingers through it, but where Tripp's was curly and long, Jake's was straight with a faded buzz on the sides. His bootcut jeans fit well and the t-shirt he wore with the magazine's logo on the back and left chest pocket fit snugly. His attention was on the arena, watching the bucking broncos.

"I'm surprised he wasn't signing autographs," Tripp said quietly as they approached Jake.

Aria's brows wrinkled with confusion, her hands tucked in the back pockets of her jeans.

"He's in the band we just heard on the radio on our way here."

"Oh, wow! That's exciting!"

Tripp patted Jake's shoulder, in hopes it was Jake since they had only met in person once prior.

"Hey, Tripp!" Jake's hand met Tripp's for a manly shake.

"Good to see ya. It's been a while," Tripp said with a nod.

"Too long, man. How ya been?"

"Good. You?"

"Great! Yeah, doin' good. Staying busy, as usual."

"Is that a wedding band on your finger? You didn't have that last time I saw ya," Tripp inquired.

"Yep, sure is. Who knew I'd settle down, right?" Jake chuckled then turned his attention to Aria.

"Who's this?" Jake asked with a suave smile.

"This is Aria." Tripp introduced her and wrapped an arm around her waist.

Jake shook her hand. "Pleasure to meet you, Aria."

"Likewise."

"The band still going strong?"

"Yeah, of course. There's no givin' that up. No matter how busy Sawyer is, he's a creature of habit. He enjoys it too much."

"I bet he is busy too, having twins now, and the therapy program on top of work and the band."

"He sure is. Owning the bar too, and that place has been booming. The girls are getting big fast, they're almost three now. Stormy is a go-getter handful smartass like her dad and a total daddy's girl. Summer is calm, sweet, and stubborn like Marina. They're already running the grandparents ragged too. They call me Uncle Jake and that's the best thing ever. Sawyer is a lucky guy all around. I'm pretty lucky too. Becka and I tied the knot, but the whole kid thing can wait a year or so." Jake laughed. "The magazine is doing great. Sawyer provides content for it so their therapy program has grown a lot."

"Sounds like everyone is doing great. I'm proud to be working for you. You have a good thing going and work with some great people."

"Thanks, Tripp. That means a lot. Without you traveling to get content for it, it wouldn't be doing nearly as well. You hand over some good shit."

Tripp chuckled. "Thanks, I'm glad you approve. Teamwork makes the dream work."

"Absolutely. How's the travel journal coming along for this issue?"

"You'll have some good shit to put in it." He chuckled. "Aria has taken a liking to scenic photography."

"Oh, yeah? Ya any good?" Jake asked, arms crossed.

She shrugged and handed over the camera. Jake scanned

through about a dozen then asked, "You took these?" before handing it back to her.

"I did. Probably not as professional as what Tripp has taken." She took the camera.

"I beg to differ. Those are fantastic," Jake said enthusiastically.

"Really?" She looked at him, then at Tripp, who nodded in agreement.

"Our photographer retired and moved to the Caribbean, so we had to pawn some of the workload off onto poor Tripp, at least for this issue. I'm glad you can help him out."

"I've been enjoying it too. I could get used to having a job like this. Tripp has it made." Aria elbowed Tripp's arm and flashed a smile.

Tripp raised a brow and nodded to Jake, who got the hint loud and clear.

"Well, I mean, if you're serious about being a photographer, show me what you can do on the rest of this travel route with Tripp. The job is yours if you want it."

"It would take a load off of me. I have all these blogs and reviews and columns to write, so..."

"I wouldn't want to mess up though. Ya know, not do well enough for the pics to be published."

"Are you kidding? The ones you've already taken are great," Tripp encouraged.

"They look professional to me. Magazine worthy." Jake shrugged, hands in his back pockets. "Tripp can check them as you go. I trust him."

"Sure, but I'm no professional either. I don't mind filling in until you find a replacement though, and I'd be thrilled being able to have Aria as my new travel companion." Tripp smiled at her. Aria's cheeks felt warm with flattery.

"It's fine by me," Jake said.

"Wait. Are you offering me a chance to prove myself or a job?" she asked Jake, unclear.

"Both. Unless you already have a job where you can't travel."

"I'm quitting! I mean, I plan to quit when I return home. I just can't do it anymore."

Tripp and Jake looked at her, then at each other.

"Seriously, I'm so ready to leave that job and do something new and exciting. I have loved this journey with you, Tripp, and I think we would work well together. Unless I'd be stepping on your toes."

"No! If Jake is willing to give you a shot and hire you as the new photographer, I think you should take him up on it. He really is great to work for and I can tell you're enjoying yourself. The sparkle in your eye glows brighter every day. And for the record, I'd be perfectly fine with you stepping on my toes." Tripp smiled and shot her a wink.

"There ya have it. You've gained experience, can dabble in your hobby, and have a new job. Boom!" Jake fist bumped Aria, but she dashed to him for a hug.

"Thanks for giving me a shot, Jake. I really appreciate it. I feel so much better now, having a plan for when I quit my job."

"No problem."

"Yeah, thanks. Makes my load lighter," Tripp chimed in.

"Ooh! Pancho is up!" Jake's attention quickly turned to the clay arena.

"Is that a bull?" Aria asked, adjusting the camera lens.

"Oh yeah! He's popular around here. I've featured him in the magazine once before. He's a beast! Nasty thing too!" Jake was excited.

"Do we take a seat? It looks pretty packed..." Tripp turned, looking at the crowded bleacher seating, which was packed full.

"Na, we can stay right here." Jake leaned an arm on the metal rail as Tripp stepped up next to him and Aria beside Tripp, camera ready. The crowd roared and the bleachers thundered with stomping feet.

"Seems like that would anger the animals more," Tripp said.

"Yeah, they don't normally allow that," Jake turned to the crowd, waving his arms and motioning for the crowd to quiet down, but a buzzer went off and out flew Pancho, a huge brown bull, beefy and powerful. Steam clouds huffing and snot dripping from Panchos wide nostrils was already impressive. He bucked so hard right out of the gate that the bull rider flew off, hitting the dirt hard and barely escaping trampling hooves. Pancho didn't even go for the red flag, he barreled straight for a clown that was headed in the direction of Jake, Tripp, and Aria. Atlas darted sideways several feet; tail nub tucked. The clown leaped to the top of the wall, trying to climb over it, but Pancho busted through the wooden arena wall, right next to the gate where the three of them stood. The clown was flung to the ground, the wooden wall on top of him. Tripp pulled Aria out of the way just in time, the three of them pinning themselves along the gate out of the way. Pounding hooves kicked up a cloud of dirt, making visibility almost impossible for several seconds as the crowd scattered, allowing the fit-throwing bull to run.

"You guys okay?" Jake hollered over the screaming crowd.

"I think so. Aria, are you okay?" Tripp frantically looked her over for any possible injuries then cupped her face in his hands, his wide eyes looking into hers.

She nodded. "Yeah. Thanks to you."

"These walls are supposed to be unbreachable. Holy shit!" Jake inspected the section of the missing wall, perplexed, before he realized the clown was under the wall. Jake and Tripp rushed to push the wall off of the clown and helped him to his feet.

"Thank you once again for saving me, Tripp." Aria took his arm in hers, squeezing it, but he brought her in for a big relieved hug. He huffed a long exhale, his chin resting on her head.

"Never a dull moment—at home *or* on the road," Jake said, shielding the sun from his eyes as he looked over the crowd to see if anyone seemed injured from where he stood.

"I hear that!" Aria agreed.

"Okay, that was *too* much action," Tripp shook his head with a chuckle.

"Shit, I need a beer after that. Hope you got that on video."

Jake laughed. "Let's go celebrate our new employee joining the crew with a cold beer on me. I have paperwork for ya to sign too."

"Sounds good, thanks," Tripp patted Jake's shoulder before he mumbled to Aria, bumping her elbow with his. "You jinxed our day going without a hitch." She playfully shoved him, making him laugh.

Atlas followed, repeatedly looking back, watching for the rogue bull.

Mile Marker 22: Biloxi

There weren't any shows playing at Varsity Theatre on their way through Baton Rouge, so they kept driving. For such a popular city, there was nothing to do. Biloxi would be the next stop.

"You wouldn't happen to have packed a really nice dress, would you?" Tripp asked.

She looked down at the country-style, mid-calf ruffled dress she was wearing then back up at him.

"Not that that one isn't nice...because it is." He was tripping over his words.

"You mean formal?" she asked, trying not to laugh at his sudden nervousness.

"Yeah, not like really formal, but..."

"Semi-formal?"

"Yeah."

"I don't think so. Why?"

"Yeah, me either." He had an idea and she could read it in his expression.

"How do you feel about a shopping excursion? I think I'll wear a suit, so whatever you find appropriate."

"You know your way to a girl's heart. You know that?" She took his hand. He laughed and added, "Shopping and coffee."

"See...and the saying goes that women are too difficult for men to figure out, but I think you've figured it out."

"I sure hope so. I underestimated how difficult it is to find semi-formal shops around here." Tripp pulled into the parking lot of a small mall as they entered Biloxi.

"I underestimated the number of firework stands." Aria pointed at one across the highway, making Tripp laugh.

"Well, we are getting closer to Alabama." Tripp exited the Jeep laughing.

"True." Aria stepped out but stopped as she shut the door. "What about Atlas?"

"I doubt we'll be that long. I left the Jeep running so he stays cool. He'll be okay if we hustle. Here." Tripp handed her a credit card.

"What's this for? I can buy my dress, Tripp. I don't want you getting in trouble for using the company card for this."

"I appreciate that, but this is actually my card. You take my credit card, I'll have my debit card. Buy whatever you'd like. Heels too." He held it out again for her to take, which she did with hesitancy.

"You're the first woman I've dated who hesitated when I handed my card over." He chuckled.

"Well, I don't like to take advantage."

"That's a great quality too, but I want you to take it."

"Just this once. I won't go crazy with it either, I promise."

"I trust you. Really though. Buy whatever you want. I want to treat you."

She started to step away from him, letting go of his hand, and said, "I've never just been handed a card before."

"Have fun." He nodded with a wide grin before turning and heading to a men's store.

Not thirty minutes later, Tripp was walking to the Jeep to wait when Aria came up behind him, shopping bag handles in her hand and the bag clunking against her leg. She wrapped an arm around him.

"I bet you thought I would take forever, didn't you?"

"Most women do. I'm impressed." He laughed, opening her door.

"Lucky for you, I like coffee much more than shopping." She slapped his firm rear playfully before getting into the Jeep. Shaking his head with a chuckle, he shut the door, then got into the driver's side. She handed his card back to him and he just looked at her for a moment.

"I've never had anyone hand my card back to me so quickly." His facial expression was blank.

"Well, I don't need it anymore. I mean, unless..." She giggled as he took it from her with a smile.

"So, what did you buy? Let's see it."

"Nope. You can wait."

"Seriously?" There was disappointment in his voice and his head tilted.

"I'm totally serious. You planning to show me yours? Because I'll show you mine if you show me yours." She bit the inside of her cheek, refraining from laughing as she looked at him.

"I mean, I can."

She shook her head no and looked away then back at him with a snicker.

"Did you at least pick out jewelry?"

"I don't need any. The necklace you bought me will look perfect with the dress I bought." She fiddled with the pendant around her neck and he gave her the biggest smile.

"Shoes?"

"I found the perfect heels. And they were on clearance. Score!" She sounded excited and his jaw dropped, dumbfounded.

"You did say I could buy shoes, right?" she asked cautiously.

"Uh..."

"Shoot. I'm sorry."

"No, no, no it's fine. I don't care what you spent. I just...I... you're a bargain shopper."

"Of course." She threw out a shrug but was confused as to what the issue was. She just kept her eyes on him as he drove."

"You're a keeper," he said after a moment of silence. The two of them had a good laugh. Teasing makes the heart grow fonder after all.

"Are we skipping dinner?" Aria checked the time on the dash.

"Nope."

"Is it part of your plan?" she asked, with a wide exaggerated grin.

"Yep." He pulled into a hotel where they hauled up their luggage and changed their clothes. She curled her light-brown hair and applied fresh makeup; her cheeks pinker than natural and light-pink lipstick to go with the slim-fitting, light-pink sequined, thin-strapped dress she wore. Strappy gold heels set the whole outfit. She tucked her little gold shimmery clutch, which held essentials, under her arm, took a deep breath, and stepped out of the bathroom. Tripp was fixing the cuff of his dress shirt under the edge of his jacket sleeve and looking out the full-length window. He saw her reflection and whipped around as she walked toward him. Her slow-spreading smile was uncontrollable as he looked so handsome in that black tux. A gold square stuck out from the breast pocket and his black shoes reflected the dim lighting of the hotel room. His dark hair was perfect and curly, and the look on his face after seeing her was wide eyed and loose lipped. His breath hitched. She set her clutch on the bed and took hold of the lapels of his suit. Their eyes locked and his sharp inhale proved she had taken his breath away. He forgot to breathe for a moment every time she would walk into the room, but this time was different.

"You clean up nicely." That flirty upward gaze she gave made it difficult for him to swallow. He cleared his throat and said, "Thanks, and you...you look absolutely stunning, Aria."

"I do?" She looked down at herself, then up at her reflection in the large window.

"Yes, you do." He wrapped his hands around her waist from behind, joining her in marveling at how they looked dressed up together.

"I guess I don't look too bad for the bargains I found." She turned to him and winked, arms up around his neck.

"You look incredible. You're the most beautiful thing I've ever seen."

"Thanks, so do you."

"Yeah?"

"Yeah. Very handsome." She pulled him closer to her. "So sexy," she whispered in his ear, sending a chill up the back of his neck.

"I can't wait to take this dress off of you when the night ends."

"Then that's not where the night shall end."

Their gazes met a brief moment before his lips melted to hers.

With Atlas left at the hotel, free to snooze all cozy on the king-sized bed, Tripp and Aria made their way to the Scarlet Pearl Casino. They walked arm-in-arm along the palm-lined sidewalk, the bright lights of the mini-Vegas on water glowing brightly as darkness fell upon the evening. Purple orchid art pieces hung from the ceiling, matching the drapes, rug, and velvety chairs at the slot machines. The place was busy; crowds gathered at card tables, slot machines ringing loudly with each pull, the occasional cheering and excited chatter mixed with clinking of coins.

"What do ya think? Wanna roll the dice?" he asked as they stood, debating on where to begin.

"You much of a gambler?" she asked, looking around.

"Well, I took a gamble pulling off to the side of the road to help change a tire for a beautiful woman once." They began walking, a smile on her face.

"True."

"You?"

"Well, there was this one time when I ventured out on a limb and agreed to ride across the country with a stranger."

"That worked out though, I'd say." He squeezed her arm in his.

"It sure did." She landed a peck on his freshly groomed cheek and took him by the hand, pulling him toward a craps table, him chuckling as he followed.

"I must warn you, I have no idea how to play most table games." She stood at an open space that cleared out as they approached. With his gentle hand on the small of her back, he smiled wide.

"I'll teach you. Just be my good luck charm."

"I'd love to say that sounds easy, but you've seen my luck. It's safer to say that you're lucky."

"Well, I'm lucky because I have you." He kissed her pink lips before holding the dice out for her to blow, her eyes narrow with uncertainty whether he was bluffing or not.

"Just follow my lead," he advised.

"I'd follow you anywhere, Tripp."

"And I hope you always will," he replied, wrapping her up in a hug before she blew on the dice again. It worked like a charm the first time. He noticed many eyes on her around the table, and even more from leering passers-by, but she paid them no attention. She only had eyes for Tripp. He cleaned up impeccably. He was so suave and handsome, with perfect posture, most impressive in every way. She looked like a movie star under that chandelier glow; absolutely marvelous. He looked at her, at the stars in her eyes, and told her he thought she was perfect. They walked arm-in-arm into the Beau Rivage Casino. Walking across the vibrant palm-print carpet, Aria mentioned she was getting hungry.

Upon being guided to their table in the fanciest restaurant she'd ever seen, he pulled out her chair and she tucked her dress beneath her as she sat.

"I can't say I've ever experienced fine dining like this before," Aria mentioned, looking around the room with the drink menu in her hand. Tripp sat, straightening his jacket. The waiter came to the table and Aria asked Tripp if they could order champagne.

"Of course. We'll take your best."

"Yes, sir," the waiter nodded before leaving the table.

"The best, huh? I didn't mean expensive."

Tripp smiled. "Only the best will do for you. I've been wanting to take you out on a fancy date, so we're going all out tonight." He took her hand on the tabletop.

"I just want to make sure you know I don't need fancy things. Not often anyways." She winked at him with a sideways smile.

"Well, you deserve it. Out of all the places we've been these last few weeks, and all the time we spent together, we needed to have an actual date."

"Every single day has felt like a date. I'm thankful for the time we've spent together, all of our adventures...most of which I would've never experienced in my lifetime without having met you. You've changed me, Tripp."

"How so?"

"I'm not so scared to try new things anymore. I'm braver than I used to be. I feel as though I've lived, you know. Of course, I was terrified doing half of those things, but I'm glad you pushed me out of my comfort zone and I don't regret a single one. This is what life is about. This whole vacation has been exactly what I've needed. I've done more than I had planned and meeting you...I didn't know I needed someone like you in my life either, but I can't say I've ever been happier."

"Really? Never?"

She shook her head. "No. Not ever."

"I'm glad to hear it because I feel the same about you and our road trip together." His gaze drifted to their hands.

"Tell me it doesn't stop when the road ends, Aria." His gaze met hers, a flash of worry in his eyes. She leaned into the table, taking his other hand in hers.

"No. I don't want this to end, Tripp. Not ever. We've already agreed on that. I love you."

"I love you too."

"I can see us being on a life-long journey together, full of fun and adventures."

"And love." He kissed the top of her hand.

"And love." Her wide eyes, parted lips, and the fact that she couldn't look away for long, was a tell. She'd be a less-than-creative poker player.

"I'm betting on forever with you."

"I'll take that bet." She looked up at him with a smile.

Hard Rock Casino was their last stop for the evening. Aria insisted on a photo of the two of them by the guitar on the front of the building and she was impressed by the color-changing guitar lights on the ceiling and gold-lit guitars above the slot machines. They played slots for about an hour then visited the gift shop where he then clipped a "True South" pin onto her clutch. The golden compass designed with an anchor and guitar was another symbol of their time together.

"You're my compass when I'm lost, Tripp. Figuratively and literally. I don't know where I'd be without you."

"We would've found each other eventually. We were meant to." He tipped her chin up and let his fingertips trial down her neck to her chest. The way he gazed into her eyes and held her gaze, frozen, a portal into a whole other world that she's never known but it's one she had stepped into and had no intention of ever leaving, stole her heart. Everything about this man's existence was amazing; his love for adventure and the ways he showed his love for her. A slot machine rang loudly behind them and blue lights flashed, interrupting their moment. He took her by the hand, leading her to the counter.

"I can't believe we came out ahead tonight," she said as he cashed out.

"Only a few hundred, but I'll take that over losing. I told you you're a good luck charm."

"Came out ahead, got to dress up, had a lovely night out together. Perfect. Thank you."

He turned to her, taking her hand. "You're welcome. Even if we hadn't walked out of here with more than we spent, I'd still have won."

"How do you figure?" she asked.

"Not only did we have an amazing time with each other, but I won the girl. You're perfect. Oh, and the night isn't over yet." He kissed her cheek.

"Mmm." She pulled him to her, arms wrapped around his neck.

"I can't wait for that part either, but first, I have a surprise for you."

"This whole night has been a surprise."

"Well, another surprise then."

"What is it?"

He took her hand and they walked into another room where seats were filling quickly.

"A show?" she asked as they took reserved seats up front.

"Tripp, these seats are reserved." She slid forward, looking behind her at the sign on the back of her chair.

"Yep. They're reserved for us."

She looked at him and the lights dimmed.

"Well, you remember meeting Jake at the rodeo?"

She nodded.

"His band is playing here tonight. He slipped me tickets when I got paperwork from him."

"Really?" she asked excitedly.

"Yep. Really."

"I need to get those papers that Jake gave me to sign to Sawyer while we're here. Don't let me forget. It might get the ball rolling faster." Tripp patted his chest on the left side where he was keeping the paperwork on the inside of his suit jacket.

"I'll remind you. What are the papers for?"

"The land Sawyer sold me. So that *we* can build *our* house."

She smiled with excitement. "Somewhere we can call ours."

He squeezed her hand and shot her a wink.

"The way you make me feel." Her gaze clung to his, soft and so full of love, until she took him by the face and kissed him so sweetly the room began cheering. They didn't notice. To them, they were the only two in the world. A guitar strum turned the crowd's attention to the stage and the curtains pulled open.

"Oh, I might have had Sawyer and Jake write a song for us. Another surprise. It's called *Wherever the Wind Blows*." He raised his brows and pecked her forehead.

"Oh my God! I can't wait to hear it!" She clapped her hands in excitement as the band began jamming, drawing their attention back to the stage. It was one hell of a show; a mix of original songs and covers too. They saved the special song for last.

"Wherever the Wind Blows"

(Verse 1)
I've been searching
No direction in mind
Aimlessly searching
Not knowing that I'd find
Someone like you

(Chorus)
You found yourself along the way
While traveling the beaten path
Navigating through night and day
Taking a leap of faith into forever with you
I saw it while gazing into your eyes
The way the stars map the sky
You've become my compass when I'm lost
My destination at any cost
Love has taken me
Wherever the wind blows

(Verse 2)
Running from something
I had a restless mind
Now I'm free-falling
'Cause I've been given a sign
I was sent to you

(Chorus)
You found yourself along the way
While traveling the beaten path
Navigating through night and day
Taking a leap of faith into forever
I saw it while gazing into your eyes
The way the stars map the sky
You've become my compass when I'm lost
My destination at any cost
Love has taken me
Wherever the wind blows

(Bridge)
I believe this was our destiny
Together on this journey
I'm going places with you

(Outro)
Your love will carry me
Wherever the wind blows

After the last song, Jake pointed at Tripp and told them to come around backstage. Aria wore a proud smile as Tripp wore her on his arm like a trophy. The band was putting instruments in cases but Jake was expecting the couple, so was the first to greet them.

"I'm glad you two were able to come to the show." Jake shook hands with Tripp and Aria.

"Me too. Good to see ya again."

"Likewise. Come meet the guys." Jake nodded for them to follow and gave Tripp a pat on the back.

"You two clean up nice."

"Thanks. Thanks for the tickets too. I've been trying to come up with an excuse to get Aria all dressed up." Trip squeezed her hand and received a big shy smile as a reaction.

"Of course, glad y'all came out for a fun night."

Sawyer turned and shook Tripp's hand. It was a strong handshake too.

"Hey, Tripp! Good to see ya again!"

"You too. It's been a while. You growing your hair out again?"

Sawyer took his black Stetson off long enough to run his fingers through his wavy hair. It was grown out about five inches long and wasn't buzzed on the sides like it had been the last time they met.

"Yeah, the wife says it's time." He laughed. "I'm sure by summer I'll feel like buzzing it again. Florida heat is brutal."

"I hear that. Looks good on ya."

"Thanks. Jake says you're a tremendous asset to the magazine. He brags about ya all the time. Seems like we never have much time to chat each time we see each other."

"That's true. That might change after I get going on this though," Tripp said as he took the paperwork from the inside of his jacket and handed it to Sawyer. Sawyer flipped through the pages quickly, ensuring all were signed.

"Land is being developed like crazy around our place so I've been trying to buy some up to prevent our space from being overrun by cookie-cutter suburbs. I'm excited to have y'all as neighbors though." Sawyer folded the papers in half, then again, and stuffed them in his back jeans pocket.

"Can't wait! This ball is rolling fast. I appreciate you selling a little chunk. I'm sorry, this is Aria."

"Pleasure to meet you, Aria," Sawyer shook her hand, flashing a dashing smile.

"Pleasure is mine. You guys are great up on that stage."

"Thanks. We sure like to tear it up," Sawyer said with a chuckle. Chris and Trev, the other band members, came over and introduced themselves, also being praised for their entertaining abilities.

"Seriously, I'm impressed. You guys sound great on the radio, but live in concert is impressive."

"That's great to hear. We appreciate the positive feedback, for sure," Jake agreed with Sawyer's thankful nod.

"So, Aria is going to be doing some photography for the magazine now," Jake added.

"Yeah? That's great."

"I'm excited for the change," Aria said, watching Chris pack up his drum set, but her attention went back to Sawyer when he asked what she did previously.

"I've been a pediatric nurse for several years. It's wearing on me more than I thought it would."

"I can understand that. I'm sure it has its highs and lows."

"At a specialty hospital, there are unfortunately more lows than highs. The cancer patients tug at my heart strings. Can't help but have a few favorites too."

"You wouldn't happen to know a tough kid named Luke, would you?"

"About to turn thirteen and is now a cowboy with a style much like yours?" Aria smiled, a hand on her hip.

"You're Luke's nurse?" Sawyer asked excitedly.

"I was, yes. I resigned this week, but he's been doing so great that he doesn't need me anymore. That's a good thing."

"Absolutely. Wow, well I'm honored to meet the nurse that took such great care of him. We see Luke a few days a week. He's such a great kid."

"He's like one of his own," Jake patted Sawyer's shoulder as he walked by to help Trev coil up cords.

"His mom was ill for a few months so Luke spent a lot of time at our place. She's better now, thank goodness, but it scared her.

She asked Marina and I to be Luke's godparents. As honored as we feel, we're glad she's feeling back to normal."

"Of course. Poor Luke. I had no idea. I do keep in contact with him, but he never said anything."

"I'm not surprised; he's a tough kid."

"He sure is."

"Since y'all will be my neighbors soon enough, come over and hang out with him anytime."

"Yeah? That would be amazing. Thank you. I can definitely see where his cowboy influence came from."

"And with the horses," Tripp added.

"Oh, I'd love to volunteer if you need help over there," Aria offered.

"Sure. Whenever you want. Actually, I'm wanting to hire a few folks for the program at Brandton Ranch so let me know if you'd be interested in working at the stables when y'all aren't traveling. I think you and my wife would get along great too. Can't wait to have y'all join our little 'clique' as Chris's lady calls our group of friends." Sawyer looked over at Chris and laughed but Chris just rolled his eyes and shook his head.

"I'm excited too. Y'all seem like a fun bunch." Aria giggled at their playfulness. "The ladies didn't come tonight?" she asked.

"Nah, we're driving home this evening so Marina stayed home with the girls," Sawyer answered.

"Well, I can't wait to meet her. The other ladies as well."

The stage manager stepped through the stage door and whirled his finger, signaling to the band to wrap it up.

"We'll let you guys pack up. It was nice to meet you guys. Thanks, Jake, Sawyer, for everything," Tripp shook all of their hands.

"Sawyer, thanks for taking care of Luke. He is one happy kid thanks to you." Aria gave Sawyer a hug.

"It wouldn't have been possible without you though. You're a miracle worker and he adores you," Sawyer praised her.

Tripp took Aria's hand to leave the band to their packing. On their way out, Jake hollered, "Y'all make a cute couple!"

Tripp laughed and Aria whispered, "They seem great."

"Yeah, they do."

"Would it be weird to hang out with our boss?"

"Nah, he doesn't act like a boss, really. He's not bossy at all." Tripp laughed at Jake's lack of intimidation. She watched Tripp's laugh turn into a chin-tucked grin.

"What?" Aria asked, eyes squinting. The city lights bright as they walked outside.

"I was just thinking of how badly I want to get you out of that dress and boss you around." He barely glanced at her, opening her Jeep door before going around to his own. Her jaw dropped loose, surprised at this forwardness. She found herself biting her bottom lip with anticipation as they made their way back to the hotel.

As they entered their room, his hand on the small of her back, he said, "Don't even think about taking that dress off before I get back in here from taking Atlas out." Atlas was anxious to get outside, and brought his leash to Tripp.

"Or what?" Aria teased seductively. Tripp looked up at her from hooking the leash to the dog's collar and smirked before walking out the door. She felt a wave of heat rush to her cheeks. She powdered her nose while she waited then sat on the edge of the bed, fully clothed, heels and all. Atlas came barging through the door first, Tripp eagerly following, and she leaned back on her palms, one leg crossed over the other, while Tripp unclipped the dog's leash and dropped it to the floor, his suit jacket following. He kicked off his shoes and socks as he walked toward her, her eyes following every move he made. Untucking his dress shirt from the top of his pants, he said in a low rumble, "Stand up." Without hesitation, she uncrossed her legs and stood, chin tilted upward and shoulders back as he took her by the face. Looking down at her submissive eyes looking up at him, he stood so close that her heeled toes were between his feet and her thigh was between his. She began unbuttoning his dress shirt as his lips kissed the side of her neck. Her eyes closed with the strong sensation of the tingle up her spine, feeling weak in the knees, and wanting him to demand more of her. His lips paired with hers intensely. Unbuttoning the last shirt button, she pulled open his shirt, breaking the kiss for a moment, exposing his solid chest. She took a step back to take him in but he couldn't resist scooping her close to him and smashing his lips to hers. Breaths became heavier as her fingertips slid down his pecs. He pushed her hand down his wash-board abs to the button of his pants. Her fumbling fingers unbuttoned and unzipped them. Her thumbs traced the inside edge of his pants around to his hips and gave a tug downward, only getting them halfway down his hips before he gently gathered her hair and moved it forward over her shoulder. He slowly unzipped the back of her dress, lips still locked, and slid a strap down one shoulder before trailing gentle kisses from the side of her neck to her shoulder. He pulled away from her and her eyes slowly opened to see him looking her up and down as he walked behind her. She stood still, anticipating his touch. Pulling her hair back over to the side, he unfastened her necklace and placed it on the nightstand, then picked up where he left off by undressing her, shimmying her dress down her body until it hit the floor. Left in just a pink lacy thong, she felt his gentle hands exploring her body as if they never had before. A heated kiss on the nape of her neck made her relax in submission again. He whipped her around by the arm, smashing her lips straight into his, then squeezed her ass, walking her backward to the bed as she tried to remove his pants. He finished pulling them off himself, taking his boxer briefs down with them. He had barely flung them off his second foot before Aria pushed him onto the bed. His brows raised in surprise and he couldn't contain a smile as she stepped between his knees. Grabbing a fist-full of his curly hair, she tipped his head back and brushed her swollen lips across his. His hands ran up the back of her legs, and when they reached her bare cheeks, pulled her onto his lap, forcing her to straddle him, her arms around his neck. His chest rose and fell quickly, repeatedly, more exaggerated each time, until he kissed her lips urgently. He didn't just pull her thong to the side, he ripped it completely off her. It fell to the floor, torn. Bending side-to-side, he removed her heels and let them fall, then flipped her onto her back on the bed and quickly crawled on top of her. It was difficult for her to breathe when he looked at her that way. That lingering eye contact sent a vibration through her body every time. His eyes remained open as he lowered his mouth to hers. Tongues twisted intensely as he watched how much she was enjoying this. He made her pool with wetness between her legs. She raised her knees on either side of him, signaling to him what she wanted him to do to her. She welcomed him, fully responsive, like always, with a slow moan. Her pink fingernails dug into his shoulder blades. He felt so good, as if it were the first time she'd had him. The groan he released in her ear as he kissed her neck told her he felt the same. The rhythm in which they moved together was as perfect as the chemistry between them. He took his time navigating her body with his dark eyes and his hands, planting kisses which made their mark like pins in a map. The back of his fingers would glide down her cheek as he explored her face with his gaze. His touch coasted her outer thigh, up to her hip. Relaxed with pleasure, her eyes closed. He sent a shiver down her spine, but in a different way than when her feet were too high above solid ground. Dragging his thumb across her bottom lip, the naughty look on his face wasn't the same shy guy from the beginning of their journey. She was addicted to him, to just the thought of him even. She had no idea a human could feel this way about another and hadn't experienced anything like this. They flourished in this pure love all night.

She lay beside him, arm across his chest and his fingertips running from her shoulder to her wrist, her still-heavy breath upon the crook of his neck, breathing in his earthy scent.

"You're worth every minute I've had to wait leading up to finding you," she said, looking up at him.

"I'm pretty sure *I* found *you*. And I'm determined to never let you go," he replied before kissing her forehead. She knew that was a gesture of safety and security and that's exactly how he made her feel: safe and secure with him. Their bodies fit perfectly together as she squeezed him tightly.

"I'm glad you haven't, but just so you know, I would've followed you anywhere."

Caressing her face, he turned to face her, and without saying a word, melted his lips to hers. She pushed his curls back out of their faces before wrapping her arm around his strong back. Heated kisses became deeper, his touch roaming her body, and before they knew it, they had reignited the fire they had burning moments before.

Mile Marker 23: Pensacola

She couldn't help but notice his hair frizzing in the sudden rise in coastal humidity. Early twilight hours looked good on him as he finished loading the Jeep. With windows down, their hair blowing in the breeze, and Atlas's face flapping out the back window, they made their way to their final destination. Well, the last destination that was circled on the map. This would be their last adventure before house-sharing plans would be put into motion. Conversations during the drive from Biloxi helped them agree on decor details for the interior and color pallet options for the exterior of the house and they both found themselves relieved to be on the same page as each other. Having similar tastes made decisions easy. It was a straight shot to Pensacola, then they'd veer onto the beach exit. Driving across the bridge to the beach was challenging, hence leaving Biloxi so early. A huge crowd was always expected for the air show, but this time the Thunderbirds would be joining the Blue Angels in the air for a spectacular display in the sky.

"I've never been to the air show before. I didn't want to deal with the crowd or get stuck on the bridge for hours in this traffic." Aria looked out over the water at all the boats anchored on the sound side."

"I have a friend that flies a small stunt plane and he gets me a great reserved viewing spot. He had mentioned that he's flying in the show this year. I think you'll enjoy yourself. This will be the perfect ending to our travel adventure. I hope, anyway." He mumbled that last part but she heard him. She also noticed he was nervously rubbing the palm of his hand on the thigh of his board shorts. Maybe crowd anxiety, which was totally understandable.

"I'm sure it will be perfect." She smiled sweetly and took his hand. He cracked a nervous half-smile.

"So, where's this perfect spot that we're going to be watching from?" Aria asked, her hair flowing with the beachy breeze, Jeep windows down.

"A condo here on the beach."

"Nice!"

When they reached the condo, bags were hauled inside before eating lunch then hitting the beach. She admired the way he looked in those board shorts and when he pulled his tank top off and flung it to the laid-out towel, she found herself staring.

"How about a swim?" he asked, then clapped his hands and ran for the water, Atlas barking on his heels. He and Atlas both jumped into the surf as Aria striped her suit cover-up off, landing it with his tank. Making sure her gold, triangle bikini top was tied securely in the back, she walked down to the water. Tripp popped up from beneath the surface, his soaked hair flipped back, water dripping from his tan, buff body, his shorts clinging to his thighs with one hand in a pocket. He had more than just Aria staring at him. She stopped with her feet in the water, ankle-deep, letting small waves bubble around her while she took in the sight of him. He stole her breath straight from her lungs and when she could inhale again, the air felt thick. Atlas chased the surf, in and out. Aria didn't pay attention to the fact that Tripp was wading back to her; she was in a daze, admiring him, until he shook salty water from his hair like a dog then lifted her by the waist, her chest at his chin level, her grip on his shoulders, and spun her around before lowering her for a kiss. She wrapped her arms around his neck, fingers dancing on his shoulders as the surf rushed over their feet. They had not a care in the world that there was a crowd of people surrounding them.

"You look amazing in this swimsuit, by the way," Tripp complimented, running a finger along the outer edge of the triangle.

"Do I?" she asked, playing coy. Oh, how she's managed to render him speechless so many times.

"It compliments your eyes...and everything else." He brushed her hair from her face, his wandering gaze then meeting hers. She didn't have to verbally compliment him in return, her hand running up his thigh and the other down his chest while looking at him like she could devour him was compliment enough.

"It's really hard to not pull these strings right now," he said quietly in her ear. Smiling, she pressed herself against him and said, "Speaking of what's hard..."

He laughed, keeping her held in front of him, then looked out over the water and pointed out parasailers.

"We should try parasailing sometime. Ooh! Skydiving!" He had a light in his wide eyes when he looked back at her.

"Tripp, that's where I draw the line."

"Last night you said I could do anything I wanted with you though," he reminded her with a straight face and his brows turned inward in disappointment, then burst out in a laugh when she playfully slapped his upper arm. He scooped her up sideways, her arms around his neck, and ran for the water, Atlas following. Chest deep, she wrapped her legs around him and played with his hair which was already trying to curl with the humidity. He held her there by her rear and planted a kiss on her lips, savoring the taste of sea salt. At first, they thought the crowd began cheering for them, but when a jet came screaming overhead they realized their attention should turn to the sky. She let herself down from him and they returned to ankle depth, him standing behind her, his arms around her as they watched incredible aviation talent. For the main event, the Blue Angels and Thunderbirds, they sat together on the sand. When the crowd's favorites left the sky, Tripp stood and reached for Aria's hand.

"Hmmm. I bet I know what you're thinking," she said, teasing and taking his hand as she stood.

"I doubt it," he replied, almost a nervous look on his face. His hand was trembling.

"You okay?" she asked, a feeling that something was wrong washing over her based on his expression.

"Uh, yeah."

"Do we need to go?"

"Not yet."

"We still haven't shell hunted, but if you wanna leave..." She began to worry as he just stood there and wrapped an arm around her.

"Tripp?" She looked at him and it took a minute for him to turn his attention to her from the sky.

"Oh, the show isn't over?" She pointed out a small stunt plane. "Is that your friend?"

"It should be." He looked away from her, letting out a slow exhale. The plane was flying a banner.

"Oh, it's just an advertising plane." She flopped her hand as if the aircraft wasn't part of the show. A barrel roll and smoke trick drew her attention before the banner straightened and was readable directly in front of them.

"Aww, that's sweet! I didn't think my name was that popular." She shielded her sunglass-covered eyes from the blazing sun. Tripp looked at her, confused. The banner read "Will you marry me, Aria?" He waved to the plane then took Aria by both hands, turning her toward him at the water's edge.

"Aria."

Her gleaming eyes grew huge with realization.

"Tripp?" She had surprise and excitement in her voice. Now *her* hands were shaking and nearby people had their phone cameras on the couple. He knelt to one knee and pulled a velvet box from his pocket. He opened it and water spilled out.

"Aria, that banner was for you. Will you marry me?"

"Oh my God!" She screamed and covered her mouth. Her bare feet couldn't hold still in the sand. He chuckled at her prancing around excitedly. She nodded and flung her arms around his neck as he stood, tears already streaming from her squinted eyes.

"I think that was a yes." He laughed, his arms around her.

"Yes! Yes, Tripp, I'll marry you!" she shouted before taking his face in her hands and kissing him passionately. The crowd clapped and cheered, happy for the couple. She wiped her joyful tears and asked, "Those pockets weren't for seashells, were they?" He tipped his head back laughing. "Nope." He fumbled the ring but kept hold of it.

"Whoa, can't be losing that. Might never find it."

"And this is way more precious than any sea shells." Her anxious smile made her glow with love for him. She held her left hand out, and with wiggling knees, accepted the ring proudly as he slid it onto her finger.

"Oh, Tripp...it's stunning." Her arms flew up around his neck and he kissed her smile.

"Not as stunning as you. You like it?" He relaxed with relief.

"I love it! It's perfect. When did you...?" she asked, closely inspecting the diamond on her finger.

"Flagstaff."

"Flagstaff?"

"That's why we had to separate into different shops right before we left town."

"So, you've had all of this planned since Arizona?"

"Actually..."

She raised her brows, surprised.

"Basically, since the Grand Canyon. I wanted to then but I didn't want to propose without a ring and we hadn't even said the 'love' word yet, so I didn't want to freak you out."

"Wow. You did once say you're full of surprises."

"Did this one scare you as much as the rest?" he asked, his hands slid down to her waist.

"No. For once, I'm not scared at all. I'm excited. So excited. I love that you had this all planned out. It was romantic and thoughtful."

"Did I do okay?"

"Perfect. I won't forget this, ever."

"Well, I wanted to make sure of that so I signaled to the gentleman behind us to record it on my phone."

"Really?"

Just then, the stranger approached Tripp and handed his phone back to him. Tripp thanked the man, shaking his hand.

"And I was about to be upset that the best adventure wasn't caught on video like the rest of this trip."

"Full of surprises." He winked at her and took her hands in his.

"What do ya say we celebrate with a beachside dinner, champagne and all?"

"I'd love that."

"Then maybe after a shower, we could lay on the sand on a blanket and gaze at the stars."

"A shower?" She bit her bottom lip and pulled him to her for a hug, looking up into his eyes.

"Yep. Wanna lie out here alone together in the dark tonight?"

"There's nowhere else I'd rather be."

They visited the historic Fort Pickens, scooting out of the air show beach crowd until the crowd died down. Visiting the naval fort, they learned about the history behind it, and Aria learned that she's most definitely, without question, claustrophobic.

"Now that we're back home, we can go scuba diving." He turned to her from inside a tunnel but she was back out into the light at the entrance, shaking her head no and taking deep breaths. He laughed and said, "Well, I guess cave diving is out." He followed her to the top of the brick wall, where they took a photo with a cannon. The photos they took of the weaponry and scenery, including the lighthouse along the bay, were spectacular. The black and white photos were the best. The aqua coastal water was beautiful with the white sand bluffs and sea oats.

After a shower, Aria changed into a sundress, and Tripp into shorts and a T-shirt. They then had a casual dinner at a beachside restaurant, during which they engaged in deeper conversation about their new home and future together.

"I'm looking forward to our next travel adventure already." Tripp leaned back in his chair.

"Me too. Do you get to choose your route or is it assigned to you?"

"They'll give me an idea of which region they want covered and I'll plan the trip. Don't worry, I'll consult with you." He laughed.

"Good! Maybe I'll be better prepared for the adventures, although, I know you told me to not think too much about them beforehand."

"Exactly. Where's the adventure in that? You know I'll throw a surprise or two in there somewhere. So, if we go further Northwest, maybe Utah, we could go whitewater rafting and horseback riding again. Maybe we could stay at a ranch in Montana near the Rocky Mountains. Kansas even too. Maybe we can see more twisters!"

Aria laughed. "Maybe from a distance this time." Her shoulders slumped forward as she leaned back.

"Okay, sure." Tripp shrugged with a devious smile.

"Bungy jumping or ziplining from...I don't know...something high." He had his chin tucked and was trying to hide a smirk.

"Nice try. You must have been a bird in a previous life. Maybe something not as high. Oh! Maybe on a different route, we could stay in a treehouse resort in the Appalachian Mountains during the beginning of fall so we can enjoy the pretty colors of the season. It's romantic, but not so much with girlfriends." Her smirk made him chuckle.

"I already look forward to it." He was quiet a moment before saying, "Who knew I'd find a love connection on a work trip?"

"Well, I'm thankful our paths crossed and that we're together."

"Me too. It's good to be back home, here with you. We've explored new places, as well as each other," Tripp said, standing from the table and taking her hand.

Tripp took a blanket from the back of the Jeep and spread it out on the sand when they walked down to the beach. Darkness had settled in and there wasn't a soul out there besides them. They cuddled together on a blanket beyond the sand dunes, gazing at the stars. She used his bicep as her pillow as they lay on their backs.

"I'm looking forward to relaxing for a while." She snuggled into his chest, taking in the sound of soft waves and the sea oats fluttering in the breeze.

"Me too. Even now that we're back home, we're going places." He kissed her forehead.

"Together. Always." Stars danced in her eyes with happiness.

Acknowledgments

No matter what stress and chaos get thrown at my life, I know I have writing and reading to bring me hope and joy. Once the inspiration sparks, the rest of the writing flows. I wish to share my way of thinking and creativity with readers so they can find hope and become lost in fictitious reality. Thank you, readers!

I want to thank my closest friends for being an inspiration for the supporting characters in this series.

Sandy Sansing CDJR in Milton, FL was kind enough to provide access to the Jeep featured on this cover.

Thank you to photographer Larry Schultz for digitally making this book cover vision a reality. I loved designing this cover with you. Readers, please check out https://larryschultz.com to view Larry's work as a talented photographer.

Thank you to photographer Phillip Davies for providing exclusive photos of Kyle. Our shoots are always so much fun.

On that note, thank you model Kyle Marquis, my friend, for being the perfect vision of "Tripp." Hugs!

Much Love, Marina Skye

About the Author

Marina Skye is from the country in a small southern town. She's a beach girl at heart but loves being around horses and volunteers with a local equine rescue center. As a romantic, this is where her inspiration for the book series bloomed. When she isn't writing, she's working one of several jobs and raising her two boys. She hopes her sons will grow to be respectful gentlemen just like the character in this series.

 facebook.com/MarinaSkyeNovels

 instagram.com/Marina_Skye23